T0162373

The Night-Born

The Night-Born

Jack London

MINT EDITIONS

The Night-Born was first published in 1911.

This edition published by Mint Editions 2021.

ISBN 9781513206080 | E-ISBN 9781513275253

Published by Mint Editions®

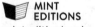
MINT
EDITIONS
minteditionbooks.com

Publishing Director: Jennifer Newens
Design & Production: Rachel Lopez Metzger
Typesetting: Westchester Publishing Services

Contents

The Night-Born

It was in the old Alta-Inyo Club—a warm night for San Francisco—and through the open windows, hushed and far, came the brawl of the streets. The talk had led on from the Graft Prosecution and the latest signs that the town was to be run wide open, down through all the grotesque sordidness and rottenness of man-hate and man-meanness, until the name of O'Brien was mentioned—O'Brien, the promising young pugilist who had been killed in the prize-ring the night before. At once the air had seemed to freshen. O'Brien had been a clean-living young man with ideals. He neither drank, smoked, nor swore, and his had been the body of a beautiful young god. He had even carried his prayer-book to the ringside. They found it in his coat pocket in the dressing-room. . . afterward.

Here was Youth, clean and wholesome, unsullied—the thing of glory and wonder for men to conjure with. . . after it has been lost to them and they have turned middle-aged. And so well did we conjure, that Romance came and for an hour led us far from the man-city and its snarling roar. Bardwell, in a way, started it by quoting from Thoreau; but it was old Trefethan, bald-headed and dewlapped, who took up the quotation and for the hour to come was romance incarnate. At first we wondered how many Scotches he had consumed since dinner, but very soon all that was forgotten.

"It was in 1898—I was thirty-five then," he said. "Yes, I know you are adding it up. You're right. I'm forty-seven now; look ten years more; and the doctors say—damn the doctors anyway!"

He lifted the long glass to his lips and sipped it slowly to soothe away his irritation.

"But I was young. . . once. I was young twelve years ago, and I had hair on top of my head, and my stomach was lean as a runner's, and the longest day was none too long for me. I was a husky back there in '98. You remember me, Milner. You knew me then. Wasn't I a pretty good bit of all right?"

Milner nodded and agreed. Like Trefethan, he was another mining engineer who had cleaned up a fortune in the Klondike.

"You certainly were, old man," Milner said. "I'll never forget when you cleaned out those lumberjacks in the M. & M. that night that little newspaper man started the row. Slavin was in the country at the time,"—this to us—"and his manager wanted to get up a match with Trefethan."

"Well, look at me now," Trefethan commanded angrily. "That's what the Goldstead did to me—God knows how many millions, but nothing left in my soul. . . nor in my veins. The good red blood is gone. I am a jellyfish, a huge, gross mass of oscillating protoplasm, a—a. . ."

But language failed him, and he drew solace from the long glass.

"Women looked at me then; and turned their heads to look a second time. Strange that I never married. But the girl. That's what I started to tell you about. I met her a thousand miles from anywhere, and then some. And she quoted to me those very words of Thoreau that Bardwell quoted a moment ago—the ones about the day-born gods and the night-born."

"It was after I had made my locations on Goldstead—and didn't know what a treasure-pot that that trip creek was going to prove—that I made that trip east over the Rockies, angling across to the Great Up North there the Rockies are something more than a back-bone. They are a boundary, a dividing line, a wall impregnable and unscalable. There is no intercourse across them, though, on occasion, from the early days, wandering trappers have crossed them, though more were lost by the way than ever came through. And that was precisely why I tackled the job. It was a traverse any man would be proud to make. I am prouder of it right now than anything else I have ever done.

"It is an unknown land. Great stretches of it have never been explored. There are big valleys there where the white man has never set foot, and Indian tribes as primitive as ten thousand years. . . almost, for they have had some contact with the whites. Parties of them come out once in a while to trade, and that is all. Even the Hudson Bay Company failed to find them and farm them.

"And now the girl. I was coming up a stream—you'd call it a river in California—uncharted—and unnamed. It was a noble valley, now shut in by high canyon walls, and again opening out into beautiful stretches, wide and long, with pasture shoulder-high in the bottoms, meadows dotted with flowers, and with clumps of timberspruce—virgin and magnificent. The dogs were packing on their backs, and were sore-footed and played out; while I was looking for any bunch of Indians to get sleds and drivers from and go on with the first snow. It was late fall, but the way those flowers persisted surprised me. I was supposed to be in sub-arctic America, and high up among the buttresses of the Rockies, and yet there was that everlasting spread of flowers. Some day the white settlers will be in there and growing wheat down all that valley.

"And then I lifted a smoke, and heard the barking of the dogs—Indian dogs—and came into camp. There must have been five hundred of them, proper Indians at that, and I could see by the jerking-frames that the fall hunting had been good. And then I met her—Lucy. That was her name. Sign language—that was all we could talk with, till they led me to a big fly—you know, half a tent, open on the one side where a campfire burned. It was all of moose-skins, this fly—moose-skins, smoke-cured, hand-rubbed, and golden-brown. Under it everything was neat and orderly as no Indian camp ever was. The bed was laid on fresh spruce boughs. There were furs galore, and on top of all was a robe of swanskins—white swan-skins—I have never seen anything like that robe. And on top of it, sitting cross-legged, was Lucy. She was nut-brown. I have called her a girl. But she was not. She was a woman, a nut-brown woman, an Amazon, a full-blooded, full-bodied woman, and royal ripe. And her eyes were blue.

"That's what took me off my feet—her eyes—blue, not China blue, but deep blue, like the sea and sky all melted into one, and very wise. More than that, they had laughter in them—warm laughter, sun-warm and human, very human, and. . . shall I say feminine? They were. They were a woman's eyes, a proper woman's eyes. You know what that means. Can I say more? Also, in those blue eyes were, at the same time, a wild unrest, a wistful yearning, and a repose, an absolute repose, a sort of all-wise and philosophical calm."

Trefethan broke off abruptly.

"You fellows think I am screwed. I'm not. This is only my fifth since dinner. I am dead sober. I am solemn. I sit here now side by side with my sacred youth. It is not I—'old' Trefethan—that talks; it is my youth, and it is my youth that says those were the most wonderful eyes I have ever seen—so very calm, so very restless; so very wise, so very curious; so very old, so very young; so satisfied and yet yearning so wistfully. Boys, I can't describe them. When I have told you about her, you may know better for yourselves."

"She did not stand up. But she put out her hand."

"'Stranger,' she said, 'I'm real glad to see you.'

"I leave it to you—that sharp, frontier, Western tang of speech. Picture my sensations. It was a woman, a white woman, but that tang! It was amazing that it should be a white woman, here, beyond the last boundary of the world—but the tang. I tell you, it hurt. It was like the stab of a flatted note. And yet, let me tell you, that woman was a poet. You shall see."

"She dismissed the Indians. And, by Jove, they went. They took her orders and followed her blind. She was hi-yu skookam chief. She told the bucks to make a camp for me and to take care of my dogs. And they did, too. And they knew enough not to get away with as much as a moccasin-lace of my outfit. She was a regular She-Who-Must-Be-Obeyed, and I want to tell you it chilled me to the marrow, sent those little thrills Marathoning up and down my spinal column, meeting a white woman out there at the head of a tribe of savages a thousand miles the other side of No Man's Land.

"'Stranger,' she said, 'I reckon you're sure the first white that ever set foot in this valley. Set down an' talk a spell, and then we'll have a bite to eat. Which way might you be comin'?'

"There it was, that tang again. But from now to the end of the yarn I want you to forget it. I tell you I forgot it, sitting there on the edge of that swan-skin robe and listening and looking at the most wonderful woman that ever stepped out of the pages of Thoreau or of any other man's book.

"I stayed on there a week. It was on her invitation. She promised to fit me out with dogs and sleds and with Indians that would put me across the best pass of the Rockies in five hundred miles. Her fly was pitched apart from the others, on the high bank by the river, and a couple of Indian girls did her cooking for her and the camp work. And so we talked and talked, while the first snow fell and continued to fall and make a surface for my sleds. And this was her story.

"She was frontier-born, of poor settlers, and you know what that means—work, work, always work, work in plenty and without end.

"'I never seen the glory of the world,' she said. 'I had no time. I knew it was right out there, anywhere, all around the cabin, but there was always the bread to set, the scrubbin' and the washin' and the work that was never done. I used to be plumb sick at times, jes' to get out into it all, especially in the spring when the songs of the birds drove me most clean crazy. I wanted to run out through the long pasture grass, wetting my legs with the dew of it, and to climb the rail fence, and keep on through the timber and up and up over the divide so as to get a look around. Oh, I had all kinds of hankerings—to follow up the canyon beds and slosh around from pool to pool, making friends with the water-dogs and the speckly trout; to peep on the sly and watch the squirrels and rabbits and small furry things and see what they was doing and learn the secrets of their ways. Seemed to me, if I had time, I could crawl among the flowers, and, if I was good and quiet, catch them whispering with themselves, telling all kinds of wise things that mere humans never know.'"

Trefethan paused to see that his glass had been refilled.

"Another time she said: 'I wanted to run nights like a wild thing, just to run through the moonshine and under the stars, to run white and naked in the darkness that I knew must feel like cool velvet, and to run and run and keep on running. One evening, plumb tuckered out—it had been a dreadful hard hot day, and the bread wouldn't raise and the churning had gone wrong, and I was all irritated and jerky—well, that evening I made mention to dad of this wanting to run of mine. He looked at me curious-some and a bit scared. And then he gave me two pills to take. Said to go to bed and get a good sleep and I'd be all hunky-dory in the morning. So I never mentioned my hankerings to him, or any one any more.'

"The mountain home broke up—starved out, I imagine—and the family came to Seattle to live. There she worked in a factory—long hours, you know, and all the rest, deadly work. And after a year of that she became waitress in a cheap restaurant—hash-slinger, she called it. She said to me once, 'Romance I guess was what I wanted. But there wan't no romance floating around in dishpans and washtubs, or in factories and hash-joints.'

"When she was eighteen she married—a man who was going up to Juneau to start a restaurant. He had a few dollars saved, and appeared prosperous. She didn't love him—she was emphatic about that, but she was all tired out, and she wanted to get away from the unending drudgery. Besides, Juneau was in Alaska, and her yearning took the form of a desire to see that wonderland. But little she saw of it. He started the restaurant, a little cheap one, and she quickly learned what he had married her for. . . to save paying wages. She came pretty close to running the joint and doing all the work from waiting to dishwashing. She cooked most of the time as well. And she had four years of it.

"Can't you picture her, this wild woods creature, quick with every old primitive instinct, yearning for the free open, and mowed up in a vile little hash-joint and toiling and moiling for four mortal years?

"'There was no meaning in anything,' she said. 'What was it all about! Why was I born! Was that all the meaning of life—just to work and work and be always tired!—to go to bed tired and to wake up tired, with every day like every other day unless it was harder?' She had heard talk of immortal life from the gospel sharps, she said, but she could not reckon that what she was doin' was a likely preparation for her immortality.

"But she still had her dreams, though more rarely. She had read a few books—what, it is pretty hard to imagine, Seaside Library novels most likely; yet they had been food for fancy. 'Sometimes,' she said, 'when I was that dizzy from the heat of the cooking that if I didn't take a breath of fresh air I'd faint, I'd stick my head out of the kitchen window, and close my eyes and see most wonderful things. All of a sudden I'd be traveling down a country road, and everything clean and quiet, no dust, no dirt; just streams ripplin' down sweet meadows, and lambs playing, breezes blowing the breath of flowers, and soft sunshine over everything; and lovely cows lazying knee-deep in quiet pools, and young girls bathing in a curve of stream all white and slim and natural— and I'd know I was in Arcady. I'd read about that country once, in a book. And maybe knights, all flashing in the sun, would come riding around a bend in the road, or a lady on a milk-white mare, and in the distance I could see the towers of a castle rising, or I just knew, on the next turn, that I'd come upon some palace, all white and airy and fairy-like, with fountains playing, and flowers all over everything, and peacocks on the lawn. . . and then I'd open my eyes, and the heat of the cooking range would strike on me, and I'd hear Jake sayin'—he was my husband—I'd hear Jake sayin', "Why ain't you served them beans? Think I can wait here all day!" Romance!—I reckon the nearest I ever come to it was when a drunken Armenian cook got the snakes and tried to cut my throat with a potato knife and I got my arm burned on the stove before I could lay him out with the potato stomper.

"'I wanted easy ways, and lovely things, and Romance and all that; but it just seemed I had no luck nohow and was only and expressly born for cooking and dishwashing. There was a wild crowd in Juneau them days, but I looked at the other women, and their way of life didn't excite me. I reckon I wanted to be clean. I don't know why; I just wanted to, I guess; and I reckoned I might as well die dishwashing as die their way."

Trefethan halted in his tale for a moment, completing to himself some thread of thought.

"And this is the woman I met up there in the Arctic, running a tribe of wild Indians and a few thousand square miles of hunting territory.

And it happened, simply enough, though, for that matter, she might have lived and died among the pots and pans. But 'Came the whisper, came the vision.' That was all she needed, and she got it.

"'I woke up one day,' she said. 'Just happened on it in a scrap of newspaper. I remember every word of it, and I can give it to you.' And then she quoted Thoreau's Cry of the Human:

"'The young pines springing up, in the corn field from year to year are to me a refreshing fact. We talk of civilizing the Indian, but that is not the name for his improvement. By the wary independence and aloofness of his dim forest life he preserves his intercourse with his native gods and is admitted from time to time to a rare and peculiar society with nature. He has glances of starry recognition, to which our saloons are strangers. The steady illumination of his qenius, dim only because distant, is like the faint but satisfying light of the stars compared with the dazzling but ineffectual and short-lived blaze of candles. The Society Islanders had their day-born gods, but they were not supposed to be of equal antiquity with the. . . night-born gods.'

"That's what she did, repeated it word for word, and I forgot the tang, for it was solemn, a declaration of religion—pagan, if you will; and clothed in the living garmenture of herself.

"'And the rest of it was torn away,' she added, a great emptiness in her voice. 'It was only a scrap of newspaper. But that Thoreau was a wise man. I wish I knew more about him.' She stopped a moment, and I swear her face was ineffably holy as she said, 'I could have made him a good wife.'

"And then she went on. 'I knew right away, as soon as I read that, what was the matter with me. I was a night-born. I, who had lived all my life with the day-born, was a night-born. That was why I had never been satisfied with cooking and dishwashing; that was why I had hankered to run naked in the moonlight. And I knew that this dirty little Juneau hash-joint was no place for me. And right there and then I said, "I quit." I packed up my few rags of clothes, and started. Jake saw me and tried to stop me.

"'What you doing?" he says.

"'Divorcin' you and me,' I says. 'I'm headin' for tall timber and where I belong.'"

"'No you don't,' he says, reaching for me to stop me. 'The cooking has got on your head. You listen to me talk before you up and do anything brash.'

"But I pulled a gun-a little Colt's forty-four—and says, 'This does my talkin' for me.'

"And I left."

Trefethan emptied his glass and called for another.

"Boys, do you know what that girl did? She was twenty-two. She had spent her life over the dish-pan and she knew no more about the world than I do of the fourth dimension, or the fifth. All roads led to her desire. No; she didn't head for the dance-halls. On the Alaskan Panhandle it is preferable to travel by water. She went down to the beach. An Indian canoe was starting for Dyea—you know the kind, carved out of a single tree, narrow and deep and sixty feet long. She gave them a couple of dollars and got on board.

"'Romance?' she told me. 'It was Romance from the jump. There were three families altogether in that canoe, and that crowded there wasn't room to turn around, with dogs and Indian babies sprawling over everything, and everybody dipping a paddle and making that canoe go.' And all around the great solemn mountains, and tangled drifts of clouds and sunshine. And oh, the silence! the great wonderful silence! And, once, the smoke of a hunter's camp, away off in the distance, trailing among the trees. It was like a picnic, a grand picnic, and I could see my dreams coming true, and I was ready for something to happen 'most any time. And it did.

"'And that first camp, on the island! And the boys spearing fish in the mouth of the creek, and the big deer one of the bucks shot just around the point. And there were flowers everywhere, and in back from the beach the grass was thick and lush and neck-high. And some of the girls went through this with me, and we climbed the hillside behind and picked berries and roots that tasted sour and were good to eat. And we came upon a big bear in the berries making his supper, and he said "Oof!" and ran away as scared as we were. And then the camp, and the camp smoke, and the smell of fresh venison cooking. It was beautiful. I was with the night-born at last, and I knew that was where I belonged. And for the first time in my life, it seemed to me, I went to bed happy that night, looking out under a corner of the canvas at the stars cut off black by a big shoulder of mountain, and listening to the night-noises, and knowing that the same thing would go on next day and forever and ever, for I wasn't going back. And I never did go back.'

"'Romance! I got it next day. We had to cross a big arm of the ocean—twelve or fifteen miles, at least; and it came on to blow when we were in the middle. That night I was along on shore, with one wolf-dog, and I was the only one left alive.'

"Picture it yourself," Trefethan broke off to say. "The canoe was wrecked and lost, and everybody pounded to death on the rocks except her. She went ashore hanging on to a dog's tail, escaping the rocks and washing up on a tiny beach, the only one in miles.

"'Lucky for me it was the mainland,' she said. 'So I headed right away back, through the woods and over the mountains and straight on anywhere. Seemed I was looking for something and knew I'd find it. I wasn't afraid. I was night-born, and the big timber couldn't kill me. And on the second day I found it. I came upon a small clearing and a tumbledown cabin. Nobody had been there for years and years. The roof had fallen in. Rotted blankets lay in the bunks, and pots and pans were on the stove. But that was not the most curious thing. Outside, along the edge of the trees, you can't guess what I found. The skeletons of eight horses, each tied to a tree. They had starved to death, I reckon, and left only little piles of bones scattered some here and there. And each horse had had a load on its back. There the loads lay, in among the bones—painted canvas sacks, and inside moosehide sacks, and inside the moosehide sacks—what do you think?'"

She stopped, reached under a corner of the bed among the spruce boughs, and pulled out a leather sack. She untied the mouth and ran out into my hand as pretty a stream of gold as I have ever seen—coarse gold, placer gold, some large dust, but mostly nuggets, and it was so fresh and rough that it scarcely showed signs of water-wash.

"'You say you're a mining engineer,' she said, 'and you know this country. Can you name a pay-creek that has the color of that gold!'

"I couldn't! There wasn't a trace of silver. It was almost pure, and I told her so.

"'You bet,' she said. 'I sell that for nineteen dollars an ounce. You can't get over seventeen for Eldorado gold, and Minook gold don't fetch quite eighteen. Well, that was what I found among the bones—eight horse-loads of it, one hundred and fifty pounds to the load.'

"'A quarter of a million dollars!' I cried out.

"'That's what I reckoned it roughly,' she answered. 'Talk about Romance! And me a slaving the way I had all the years, when as soon as I ventured out, inside three days, this was what happened. And what became of the men that mined all that gold? Often and often I wonder about it. They left their horses, loaded and tied, and just disappeared off the face of the earth, leaving neither hide nor hair behind them. I never heard tell of them. Nobody knows anything about them. Well, being the night-born, I reckon I was their rightful heir.'"

Trefethan stopped to light a cigar.

"Do you know what that girl did? She cached the gold, saving out thirty pounds, which she carried back to the coast. Then she signaled a passing canoe, made her way to Pat Healy's trading post at Dyea, outfitted, and went over Chilcoot Pass. That was in '88—eight years before the Klondike strike, and the Yukon was a howling wilderness. She was afraid of the bucks, but she took two young squaws with her, crossed the lakes, and went down the river and to all the early camps on the Lower Yukon. She wandered several years over that country and then on in to where I met her. Liked the looks of it, she said, seeing, in her own words, 'a big bull caribou knee-deep in purple iris on the valley-bottom.' She hooked up with the Indians, doctored them, gained their confidence, and gradually took them in charge. She had only left that country once, and then, with a bunch of the young bucks, she went over Chilcoot, cleaned up her gold-cache, and brought it back with her.

"'And here I be, stranger,' she concluded her yarn, 'and here's the most precious thing I own.'

"She pulled out a little pouch of buckskin, worn on her neck like a locket, and opened it. And inside, wrapped in oiled silk, yellowed with age and worn and thumbed, was the original scrap of newspaper containing the quotation from Thoreau.

"'And are you happy. . . satisfied?' I asked her. 'With a quarter of a million you wouldn't have to work down in the States. You must miss a lot.'

"'Not much,' she answered. 'I wouldn't swop places with any woman down in the States. These are my people; this is where I belong. But there are times—and in her eyes smoldered up that hungry yearning I've mentioned—'there are times when I wish most awful bad for that Thoreau man to happen along.'

"'Why?' I asked.

"'So as I could marry him. I do get mighty lonesome at spells. I'm just a woman—a real woman. I've heard tell of the other kind of women that gallivanted off like me and did queer things—the sort that become soldiers in armies, and sailors on ships. But those women are queer themselves. They're more like men than women; they look like men and they don't have ordinary women's needs. They don't want love, nor little children in their arms and around their knees. I'm not that sort. I leave it to you, stranger. Do I look like a man?'

"She didn't. She was a woman, a beautiful, nut-brown woman, with a sturdy, health-rounded woman's body and with wonderful deep-blue woman's eyes.

"'Ain't I woman?' she demanded. 'I am. I'm 'most all woman, and then some. And the funny thing is, though I'm night-born in everything else, I'm not when it comes to mating. I reckon that kind likes its own kind best. That's the way it is with me, anyway, and has been all these years.'

"'You mean to tell me—' I began.

"'Never,' she said, and her eyes looked into mine with the straightness of truth. 'I had one husband, only—him I call the Ox; and I reckon he's still down in Juneau running the hash-joint. Look him up, if you ever get back, and you'll find he's rightly named.'

"And look him up I did, two years afterward. He was all she said— solid and stolid, the Ox—shuffling around and waiting on the tables.

"'You need a wife to help you,' I said.

"'I had one once,' was his answer.

"'Widower?'

"'Yep. She went loco. She always said the heat of the cooking would get her, and it did. Pulled a gun on me one day and ran away with some Siwashes in a canoe. Caught a blow up the coast and all hands drowned.'"

Trefethan devoted himself to his glass and remained silent.

"But the girl?" Milner reminded him.

"You left your story just as it was getting interesting, tender. Did it?"

"It did," Trefethan replied. "As she said herself, she was savage in everything except mating, and then she wanted her own kind. She was very nice about it, but she was straight to the point. She wanted to marry me.

"'Stranger,' she said, 'I want you bad. You like this sort of life or you wouldn't be here trying to cross the Rockies in fall weather. It's a likely spot. You'll find few likelier. Why not settle down! I'll make you a good wife.'

"And then it was up to me. And she waited. I don't mind confessing that I was sorely tempted. I was half in love with her as it was. You know I have never married. And I don't mind adding, looking back over my life, that she is the only woman that ever affected me that way. But it was too preposterous, the whole thing, and I lied like a gentleman. I told her I was already married.

"'Is your wife waiting for you?' she asked.

"I said yes.

"'And she loves you?'

"I said yes.

"And that was all. She never pressed her point. . . except once, and then she showed a bit of fire.

"'All I've got to do,' she said, 'is to give the word, and you don't get away from here. If I give the word, you stay on. . . But I ain't going to give it. I wouldn't want you if you didn't want to be wanted. . . and if you didn't want me.'

"She went ahead and outfitted me and started me on my way.

"'It's a darned shame, stranger," she said, at parting. 'I like your looks, and I like you. If you ever change your mind, come back.'

"Now there was one thing I wanted to do, and that was to kiss her good-bye, but I didn't know how to go about it nor how she would take it.—I tell you I was half in love with her. But she settled it herself.

"'Kiss me,' she said. 'Just something to go on and remember.'

"And we kissed, there in the snow, in that valley by the Rockies, and I left her standing by the trail and went on after my dogs. I was six weeks in crossing over the pass and coming down to the first post on Great Slave Lake."

The brawl of the streets came up to us like a distant surf. A steward, moving noiselessly, brought fresh siphons. And in the silence Trefethan's voice fell like a funeral bell:

"It would have been better had I stayed. Look at me."

We saw his grizzled mustache, the bald spot on his head, the puff-sacks under his eyes, the sagging cheeks, the heavy dewlap, the general tiredness and staleness and fatness, all the collapse and ruin of a man who had once been strong but who had lived too easily and too well.

"It's not too late, old man," Bardwell said, almost in a whisper.

"By God! I wish I weren't a coward!" was Trefethan's answering cry. "I could go back to her. She's there, now. I could shape up and live many a long year. . . with her. . . up there. To remain here is to commit suicide. But I am an old man—forty-seven—look at me. The trouble is," he lifted his glass and glanced at it, "the trouble is that suicide of this sort is so easy. I am soft and tender. The thought of the long day's travel with the dogs appalls me; the thought of the keen frost in the morning and of the frozen sled-lashings frightens me—"

Automatically the glass was creeping toward his lips. With a swift surge of anger he made as if to crash it down upon the floor. Next came hesitancy and second thought. The glass moved upward to his lips and paused. He laughed harshly and bitterly, but his words were solemn:

"Well, here's to the Night-Born. She *was* a wonder."

The Madness of John Harned

I *tell* this for a fact. It happened in the bull-ring at Quito. I sat in the box with John Harned, and with Maria Valenzuela, and with Luis Cervallos. I saw it happen. I saw it all from first to last. I was on the steamer Ecuadore from Panama to Guayaquil. Maria Valenzuela is my cousin. I have known her always. She is very beautiful. I am a Spaniard— an Ecuadoriano, true, but I am descended from Pedro Patino, who was one of Pizarro's captains. They were brave men. They were heroes. Did not Pizarro lead three hundred and fifty Spanish cavaliers and four thousand Indians into the far Cordilleras in search of treasure? And did not all the four thousand Indians and three hundred of the brave cavaliers die on that vain quest? But Pedro Patino did not die. He it was that lived to found the family of the Patino. I am Ecuadoriano, true, but I am Spanish. I am Manuel de Jesus Patino. I own many haciendas, and ten thousand Indians are my slaves, though the law says they are free men who work by freedom of contract. The law is a funny thing. We Ecuadorianos laugh at it. It is our law. We make it for ourselves. I am Manuel de Jesus Patino. Remember that name. It will be written some day in history. There are revolutions in Ecuador. We call them elections. It is a good joke is it not?—what you call a pun?

John Harned was an American. I met him first at the Tivoli hotel in Panama. He had much money—this I have heard. He was going to Lima, but he met Maria Valenzuela in the Tivoli hotel. Maria Valenzuela is my cousin, and she is beautiful. It is true, she is the most beautiful woman in Ecuador. But also is she most beautiful in every country—in Paris, in Madrid, in New York, in Vienna. Always do all men look at her, and John Harned looked long at her at Panama. He loved her, that I know for a fact. She was Ecuadoriano, true—but she was of all countries; she was of all the world. She spoke many languages. She sang—ah! like an artiste. Her smile—wonderful, divine. Her eyes—ah! have I not seen men look in her eyes? They were what you English call amazing. They were promises of paradise. Men drowned themselves in her eyes.

Maria Valenzuela was rich—richer than I, who am accounted very rich in Ecuador. But John Harned did not care for her money. He had a heart—a funny heart. He was a fool. He did not go to Lima. He left the steamer at Guayaquil and followed her to Quito. She was coming home from Europe and other places. I do not see what she found in him, but she liked him. This I know for a fact, else he would not have followed her to Quito. She asked him to come. Well do I remember the occasion. She said:

"Come to Quito and I will show you the bullfight—brave, clever, magnificent!"

But he said: "I go to Lima, not Quito. Such is my passage engaged on the steamer."

"You travel for pleasure—no?" said Maria Valenzuela; and she looked at him as only Maria Valenzuela could look, her eyes warm with the promise.

And he came. No; he did not come for the bull-fight. He came because of what he had seen in her eyes. Women like Maria Valenzuela are born once in a hundred years. They are of no country and no time. They are what you call goddesses. Men fall down at their feet. They play with men and run them through their pretty fingers like sand. Cleopatra was such a woman they say; and so was Circe. She turned men into swine. Ha! ha! It is true—no?

It all came about because Maria Valenzuela said:

"You English people are—what shall I say?—savage—no? You prize-fight. Two men each hit the other with their fists till their eyes are blinded and their noses are broken. Hideous! And the other men who look on cry out loudly and are made glad. It is barbarous—no?"

"But they are men," said John Harned; "and they prize-fight out of desire. No one makes them prize-fight. They do it because they desire it more than anything else in the world."

Maria Valenzuela—there was scorn in her smile as she said: "They kill each other often—is it not so? I have read it in the papers."

"But the bull," said John Harned.

"The bull is killed many times in the bull-fight, and the bull does not come into the the ring out of desire. It is not fair to the bull. He is compelled to fight. But the man in the prize-fight—no; he is not compelled."

"He is the more brute therefore," said Maria Valenzuela.

"He is savage. He is primitive. He is animal. He strikes with his paws like a bear from a cave, and he is ferocious. But the bull-fight—ah! You have not seen the bullfight—no? The toreador is clever. He must have skill. He is modern. He is romantic. He is only a man, soft and tender, and he faces the wild bull in conflict. And he kills with a sword, a slender sword, with one thrust, so, to the heart of the great beast. It is delicious. It makes the heart beat to behold—the small man, the great beast, the wide level sand, the thousands that look on without breath; the great beast rushes to the attack, the small man stands like a statue; he does not move, he is unafraid, and in his hand is the slender sword flashing like silver in the sun; nearer and nearer rushes the great beast with its sharp horns, the man does not move, and then—so—the sword flashes, the thrust is made, to the heart, to the hilt, the bull falls to the sand and is dead, and the man is unhurt. It is brave. It is magnificent! Ah!—I could love the toreador. But the man of the prize-fight—he is the brute, the human beast, the savage primitive, the maniac that receives many blows in his stupid face and rejoices. Come to Quito and I will show you the brave sport of men, the toreador and the bull."

But John Harned did not go to Quito for the bull-fight. He went because of Maria Valenzuela. He was a large man, more broad of shoulder than we Ecuadorianos, more tall, more heavy of limb and bone. True, he was larger of his own race. His eyes were blue, though I have seen them gray, and, sometimes, like cold steel. His features were large, too—not delicate like ours, and his jaw was very strong to look at. Also, his face was smooth-shaven like a priest's. Why should a man feel shame for the hair on his face? Did not God put it there? Yes, I believe in God—I am not a pagan like many of you English. God is good. He made me an Ecuadoriano with ten thousand slaves. And when I die I shall go to God. Yes, the priests are right.

But John Harned. He was a quiet man. He talked always in a low voice, and he never moved his hands when he talked. One would have thought his heart was a piece of ice; yet did he have a streak of warm in his blood, for he followed Maria Valenzuela to Quito. Also, and for all that he talked low without moving his hands, he was an animal, as you shall see—the beast primitive, the stupid, ferocious savage of the long ago that dressed in wild skins and lived in the caves along with the bears and wolves.

Luis Cervallos is my friend, the best of Ecuadorianos. He owns three cacao plantations at Naranjito and Chobo. At Milagro is his big sugar plantation. He has large haciendas at Ambato and Latacunga, and down the coast is he interested in oil-wells. Also has he spent much money in planting rubber along the Guayas. He is modern, like the Yankee; and, like the Yankee, full of business. He has much money, but it is in many ventures, and ever he needs more money for new ventures and for the old ones. He has been everywhere and seen everything. When he was a very young man he was in the Yankee military academy what you call West Point. There was trouble. He was made to resign. He does not like Americans. But he did like Maria Valenzuela, who was of his own country. Also, he needed her money for his ventures and for his gold mine in Eastern Ecuador where the painted Indians live. I was his friend. It was my desire that he should marry Maria Valenzuela. Further, much of my money had I invested in his ventures, more so in his gold mine which was very rich but which first required the expense of much money before it would yield forth its riches. If Luis Cervallos married Maria Valenzuela I should have more money very immediately.

But John Harned followed Maria Valenzuela to Quito, and it was quickly clear to us—to Luis Cervallos and me that she looked upon John Harned with great kindness. It is said that a woman will have her will, but this is a case not in point, for Maria Valenzuela did not have her will—at least not with John Harned. Perhaps it would all have happened as it did, even if Luis Cervallos and I had not sat in the box that day at the bull-ring in Quito. But this I know: we *did* sit in the box that day. And I shall tell you what happened.

The four of us were in the one box, guests of Luis Cervallos. I was next to the Presidente's box. On the other side was the box of General Jose Eliceo Salazar. With him were Joaquin Endara and Urcisino Castillo, both generals, and Colonel Jacinto Fierro and Captain Baltazar de Echeverria. Only Luis Cervallos had the position and the influence to get that box next to the Presidente. I know for a fact that the Presidente himself expressed the desire to the management that Luis Cervallos should have that box.

The band finished playing the national hymn of Ecuador. The procession of the toreadors was over. The Presidente nodded to begin. The bugles blew, and the bull dashed in—you know the way, excited, bewildered, the darts in its shoulder burning like fire, itself seeking madly whatever enemy to destroy. The toreadors hid behind their shelters and waited. Suddenly they appeared forth, the capadores, five of them, from every side, their colored capes flinging wide. The bull paused at sight of such a generosity of enemies, unable in his own mind to know which to attack. Then advanced one of the capadors alone to meet the bull. The bull was very angry. With its fore-legs it pawed the sand of the arena till the dust rose all about it. Then it charged, with lowered head, straight for the lone capador.

It is always of interest, the first charge of the first bull. After a time it is natural that one should grow tired, trifle, that the keenness should lose its edge. But that first charge of the first bull! John Harned was seeing it for the first time, and he could not escape the excitement—the sight of the man, armed only with a piece of cloth, and of the bull rushing upon him across the sand with sharp horns, widespreading.

"See!" cried Maria Valenzuela. "Is it not superb?"

John Harned nodded, but did not look at her. His eyes were sparkling, and they were only for the bull-ring. The capador stepped to the side, with a twirl of the cape eluding the bull and spreading the cape on his own shoulders.

"What do you think?" asked Maria Venzuela. "Is it not a—what-you-call—sporting proposition—no?"

"It is certainly," said John Harned. "It is very clever."

She clapped her hands with delight. They were little hands. The audience applauded. The bull turned and came back. Again the capadore eluded him, throwing the cape on his shoulders, and again the audience applauded. Three times did this happen. The capadore was very excellent. Then he retired, and the other capadore played with the bull. After that they placed the banderillos in the bull, in the shoulders, on each side of the back-bone, two at a time. Then stepped forward Ordonez, the chief matador, with the long sword and the scarlet cape. The bugles blew for the death. He is not so good as Matestini. Still he is good, and with one thrust he drove the sword to the heart, and the bull doubled his legs under him and lay down and died. It was a pretty thrust, clean and sure; and there was much applause, and many of the common people threw their hats into the ring. Maria Valenzuela clapped her hands with the rest, and John Harned, whose cold heart was not touched by the event, looked at her with curiosity.

"You like it?" he asked.

"Always," she said, still clapping her hands.

"From a little girl," said Luis Cervallos. "I remember her first fight. She was four years old. She sat with her mother, and just like now she clapped her hands. She is a proper Spanish woman.

"You have seen it," said Maria Valenzuela to John Harned, as they fastened the mules to the dead bull and dragged it out. "You have seen the bull-fight and you like it—no? What do you think?

"I think the bull had no chance," he said. "The bull was doomed from the first. The issue was not in doubt. Every one knew, before the bull entered the ring, that it was to die. To be a sporting proposition, the issue must be in doubt. It was one stupid bull who had never fought a man against five wise men who had fought many bulls. It would be possibly a little bit fair if it were one man against one bull."

"Or one man against five bulls," said Maria Valenzuela; and we all laughed, and Luis Ceryallos laughed loudest.

"Yes," said John Harned, "against five bulls, and the man, like the bulls, never in the bull ring before—a man like yourself, Senor Crevallos."

"Yet we Spanish like the bull-fight," said Luis Cervallos; and I swear the devil was whispering then in his ear, telling him to do that which I shall relate.

"Then must it be a cultivated taste," John Harned made answer. "We kill bulls by the thousand every day in Chicago, yet no one cares to pay admittance to see."

"That is butchery," said I; "but this—ah, this is an art. It is delicate. It is fine. It is rare."

"Not always," said Luis Cervallos. "I have seen clumsy matadors, and I tell you it is not nice."

He shuddered, and his face betrayed such what-you-call disgust, that I knew, then, that the devil was whispering and that he was beginning to play a part.

"Senor Harned may be right," said Luis Cervallos. "It may not be fair to the bull. For is it not known to all of us that for twenty-four hours the bull is given no water, and that immediately before the fight he is permitted to drink his fill?"

"And he comes into the ring heavy with water?" said John Harned quickly; and I saw that his eyes were very gray and very sharp and very cold.

"It is necessary for the sport," said Luis Cervallos. "Would you have the bull so strong that he would kill the toreadors?"

"I would that he had a fighting chance," said John Harned, facing the ring to see the second bull come in.

It was not a good bull. It was frightened. It ran around the ring in search of a way to get out. The capadors stepped forth and flared their capes, but he refused to charge upon them.

"It is a stupid bull," said Maria Valenzuela.

"I beg pardon," said John Harned; "but it would seem to me a wise bull. He knows he must not fight man. See! He smells death there in the ring."

True. The bull, pausing where the last one had died, was smelling the wet sand and snorting. Again he ran around the ring, with raised head, looking at the faces of the thousands that hissed him, that threw orange-peel at him and called him names. But the smell of blood decided him, and he charged a capador, so without warning that the man just escaped. He dropped his cape and dodged into the shelter. The bull struck the wall of the ring with a crash. And John Harned said, in a quiet voice, as though he talked to himself:

"I will give one thousand sucres to the lazar-house of Quito if a bull kills a man this day."

"You like bulls?" said Maria Valenzuela with a smile.

"I like such men less," said John Harned. "A toreador is not a brave man. He surely cannot be a brave man. See, the bull's tongue is already out. He is tired and he has not yet begun."

"It is the water," said Luis Cervallos.

"Yes, it is the water," said John Harned. "Would it not be safer to hamstring the bull before he comes on?"

Maria Valenzuela was made angry by this sneer in John Harned's words. But Luis Cervallos smiled so that only I could see him, and then it broke upon my mind surely the game he was playing. He and I were to be banderilleros. The big American bull was there in the box with us. We were to stick the darts in him till he became angry, and then there might be no marriage with Maria Valenzuela. It was a good sport. And the spirit of bull-fighters was in our blood.

The bull was now angry and excited. The capadors had great game with him. He was very quick, and sometimes he turned with such sharpness that his hind legs lost their footing and he plowed the sand with his quarter. But he charged always the flung capes and committed no harm.

"He has no chance," said John Harned. "He is fighting wind."

"He thinks the cape is his enemy," explained Maria Valenzuela. "See how cleverly the capador deceives him."

"It is his nature to be deceived," said John Harned. "Wherefore he is doomed to fight wind. The toreadors know it, you know it, I know it—we all know from the first that he will fight wind. He only does not know it. It is his stupid beast-nature. He has no chance."

"It is very simple," said Luis Cervallos. "The bull shuts his eyes when he charges. Therefore—"

"The man steps, out of the way and the bull rushes by," Harned interrupted.

"Yes," said Luis Cervallos; "that is it. The bull shuts his eyes, and the man knows it."

"But cows do not shut their eyes," said John Harned. "I know a cow at home that is a Jersey and gives milk, that would whip the whole gang of them."

"But the toreadors do not fight cows," said I.

"They are afraid to fight cows," said John Harned.

"Yes," said Luis Cervallos, "they are afraid to fight cows. There would be no sport in killing toreadors."

"There would be some sport," said John Harned, "if a toreador were killed once in a while. When I become an old man, and mayhap a cripple, and should I need to make a living and be unable to do hard work, then would I become a bull-fighter. It is a light vocation for elderly gentlemen and pensioners."

"But see!" said Maria Valenzuela, as the bull charged bravely and the capador eluded it with a fling of his cape. "It requires skill so to avoid the beast."

"True," said John Harned. "But believe me, it requires a thousand times more skill to avoid the many and quick punches of a prize-fighter who keeps his eyes open and strikes with intelligence. Furthermore, this bull does not want to fight. Behold, he runs away."

It was not a good bull, for again it ran around the ring, seeking to find a way out.

"Yet these bulls are sometimes the most dangerous," said Luis Cervallos. "It can never be known what they will do next. They are wise. They are half cow. The bull-fighters never like them.—See! He has turned!"

Once again, baffled and made angry by the walls of the ring that would not let him out, the bull was attacking his enemies valiantly.

"His tongue is hanging out," said John Harned. "First, they fill him with water. Then they tire him out, one man and then another, persuading him to exhaust himself by fighting wind. While some tire him, others rest. But the bull they never let rest. Afterward, when he is quite tired and no longer quick, the matador sticks the sword into him."

The time had now come for the banderillos. Three times one of the fighters endeavored to place the darts, and three times did he fail. He but stung the bull and maddened it. The banderillos must go in, you know, two at a time, into the shoulders, on each side the backbone and close to it. If but one be placed, it is a failure. The crowd hissed and called for Ordonez. And then Ordonez did a great thing. Four times he stood forth, and four times, at the first attempt, he stuck in the banderillos, so that eight of them, well placed, stood out of the back of the bull at one time. The crowd went mad, and a rain of hats and money fell on the sand of the ring.

And just then the bull charged unexpectedly one of the capadors. The man slipped and lost his head. The bull caught him—fortunately, between his wide horns. And while the audience watched, breathless and silent, John Harned stood up and yelled with gladness. Alone, in that hush of all of us, John Harned yelled. And he yelled for the bull. As you see yourself, John Harned wanted the man killed. His was a brutal heart. This bad conduct made those angry that sat in the box of General Salazar, and they cried out against John Harned. And Urcisino Castillo told him to his face that he was a dog of a Gringo and other things. Only it was in Spanish, and John Harned did not understand. He stood and yelled, perhaps for the time of ten seconds, when the bull was enticed into charging the other capadors and the man arose unhurt.

"The bull has no chance," John Harned said with sadness as he sat down. "The man was uninjured. They fooled the bull away from him." Then he turned to Maria Valenzuela and said: "I beg your pardon. I was excited."

She smiled and in reproof tapped his arm with her fan.

"It is your first bull-fight," she said. "After you have seen more you will not cry for the death of the man. You Americans, you see, are more brutal than we. It is because of your prize-fighting. We come only to see the bull killed."

"But I would the bull had some chance," he answered. "Doubtless, in time, I shall cease to be annoyed by the men who take advantage of the bull."

The bugles blew for the death of the bull. Ordonez stood forth with the sword and the scarlet cloth. But the bull had changed again, and did not want to fight. Ordonez stamped his foot in the sand, and cried out, and waved the scarlet cloth. Then the bull charged, but without heart. There was no weight to the charge. It was a poor thrust. The sword struck a bone and bent. Ordonez took a fresh sword. The bull, again stung to fight, charged once more. Five times Ordonez essayed the thrust, and each time the sword went but part way in or struck bone. The sixth time, the sword went in to the hilt. But it was a bad thrust. The sword missed the heart and stuck out half a yard through the ribs on the opposite side. The audience hissed the matador. I glanced at John Harned. He sat silent, without movement; but I could see his teeth were set, and his hands were clenched tight on the railing of the box.

All fight was now out of the bull, and, though it was no vital thrust, he trotted lamely what of the sword that stuck through him, in one side and out the other. He ran away from the matador and the capadors, and circled the edge of the ring, looking up at the many faces.

"He is saying: 'For God's sake let me out of this; I don't want to fight,'" said John Harned.

That was all. He said no more, but sat and watched, though sometimes he looked sideways at Maria Valenzuela to see how she took it. She was angry with the matador. He was awkward, and she had desired a clever exhibition.

The bull was now very tired, and weak from loss of blood, though far from dying. He walked slowly around the wall of the ring, seeking a way out. He would not charge. He had had enough. But he must be killed. There is a place, in the neck of a bull behind the horns, where the cord of the spine is unprotected and where a short stab will immediately kill. Ordonez stepped in front of the bull and lowered his scarlet cloth to the ground. The bull would not charge. He stood still and smelled the cloth, lowering his head to do so. Ordonez stabbed between the horns at the spot in the neck. The bull jerked his head up. The stab had missed. Then the bull watched the sword. When Ordonez moved the cloth on the ground, the bull forgot the sword and lowered his head to smell the cloth. Again Ordonez stabbed, and again he failed. He tried many times. It was stupid. And John Harned said nothing. At last a stab went home, and the bull fell to the sand, dead immediately, and the mules were made fast and he was dragged out.

"The Gringos say it is a cruel sport—no?" said Luis Cervallos. "That it is not humane. That it is bad for the bull. No?"

"No," said John Harned. "The bull does not count for much. It is bad for those that look on. It is degrading to those that look on. It teaches them to delight in animal suffering. It is cowardly for five men to fight one stupid bull. Therefore those that look on learn to be cowards. The bull dies, but those that look on live and the lesson is learned. The bravery of men is not nourished by scenes of cowardice."

Maria Valenzuela said nothing. Neither did she look at him. But she heard every word and her cheeks were white with anger. She looked out across the ring and fanned herself, but I saw that her hand trembled.

Nor did John Harned look at her. He went on as though she were not there. He, too, was angry, coldly angry.

"It is the cowardly sport of a cowardly people," he said.

"Ah," said Luis Cervallos softly, "you think you understand us."

"I understand now the Spanish Inquisition," said John Harned. "It must have been more delightful than bull-fighting."

Luis Cervallos smiled but said nothing. He glanced at Maria Valenzuela, and knew that the bull-fight in the box was won. Never would she have further to do with the Gringo who spoke such words. But neither Luis Cervallos nor I was prepared for the outcome of the day. I fear we do not understand the Gringos. How were we to know that John Harned, who was so coldly angry, should go suddenly mad! But mad he did go, as you shall see. The bull did not count for much— he said so himself. Then why should the horse count for so much? That I cannot understand. The mind of John Harned lacked logic. That is the only explanation.

"It is not usual to have horses in the bull-ring at Quito," said Luis Cervallos, looking up from the program. "In Spain they always have them. But to-day, by special permission we shall have them. When the next bull comes on there will be horses and picadors-you know, the men who carry lances and ride the horses."

"The bull is doomed from the first," said John Harned. "Are the horses then likewise doomed!"

"They are blindfolded so that they may not see the bull," said Luis Cervallos. "I have seen many horses killed. It is a brave sight."

"I have seen the bull slaughtered," said John Harned "I will now see the horse slaughtered, so that I may understand more fully the fine points of this noble sport."

"They are old horses," said Luis Cervallos, "that are not good for anything else."

"I see," said John Harned.

The third bull came on, and soon against it were both capadors and picadors. One picador took his stand directly below us. I agree, it was a thin and aged horse he rode, a bag of bones covered with mangy hide.

"It is a marvel that the poor brute can hold up the weight of the rider," said John Harned. "And now that the horse fights the bull, what weapons has it?"

"The horse does not fight the bull," said Luis Cervallos.

"Oh," said John Harned, "then is the horse there to be gored? That must be why it is blindfolded, so that it shall not see the bull coming to gore it."

"Not quite so," said I. "The lance of the picador is to keep the bull from goring the horse."

"Then are horses rarely gored?" asked John Harned.

"No," said Luis Cervallos. "I have seen, at Seville, eighteen horses killed in one day, and the people clamored for more horses."

"Were they blindfolded like this horse?" asked John Harned.

"Yes," said Luis Cervallos.

After that we talked no more, but watched the fight. And John Harned was going mad all the time, and we did not know. The bull refused to charge the horse. And the horse stood still, and because it could not see it did not know that the capadors were trying to make the bull charge upon it. The capadors teased the bull their capes, and when it charged them they ran toward the horse and into their shelters. At last the bull was angry, and it saw the horse before it.

"The horse does not know, the horse does not know," John Harned whispered to himself, unaware that he voiced his thought aloud.

The bull charged, and of course the horse knew nothing till the picador failed and the horse found himself impaled on the bull's horns from beneath. The bull was magnificently strong. The sight of its strength was splendid to see. It lifted the horse clear into the air; and as the horse fell to its side on on the ground the picador landed on his feet and escaped, while the capadors lured the bull away. The horse was emptied of its essential organs. Yet did it rise to its feet screaming. It was the scream of the horse that did it, that made John Harned completely mad; for he, too, started to rise to his feet, I heard him curse low and deep. He never took his eyes from the horse, which, screaming, strove to run, but fell down instead and rolled on its back so that all its four legs were kicking in the air. Then the bull charged it and gored it again and again until it was dead.

John Harned was now on his feet. His eyes were no longer cold like steel. They were blue flames. He looked at Maria Valenzuela, and she looked at him, and in his face was a great loathing. The moment of his madness was upon him. Everybody was looking, now that the horse was dead; and John Harned was a large man and easy to be seen.

"Sit down," said Luis Cervallos, "or you will make a fool of yourself."

John Harned replied nothing. He struck out his fist. He smote Luis Cervallos in the face so that he fell like a dead man across the chairs and did not rise again. He saw nothing of what followed. But I saw much. Urcisino Castillo, leaning forward from the next box, with his cane struck John Harned full across the face. And John Harned smote him with his fist so that in falling he overthrew General Salazar. John Harned was now in what-you-call Berserker rage—no? The beast primitive in him was loose and roaring—the beast primitive of the holes and caves of the long ago.

"You came for a bull-fight," I heard him say, "And by God I'll show you a man-fight!"

It was a fight. The soldiers guarding the Presidente's box leaped across, but from one of them he took a rifle and beat them on their heads with it. From the other box Colonel Jacinto Fierro was shooting at him with a revolver. The first shot killed a soldier. This I know for a fact. I saw it. But the second shot struck John Harned in the side. Whereupon he swore, and with a lunge drove the bayonet of his rifle into Colonel Jacinto Fierro's body. It was horrible to behold. The Americans and the English are a brutal race. They sneer at our bull-fighting, yet do they delight in the shedding of blood. More men were killed that day because of John Harned than were ever killed in all the history of the bull-ring of Quito, yes, and of Guayaquil and all Ecuador.

It was the scream of the horse that did it, yet why did not John Harned go mad when the bull was killed? A beast is a beast, be it bull or horse. John Harned was mad. There is no other explanation. He was blood-mad, a beast himself. I leave it to your judgment. Which is worse—the goring of the horse by the bull, or the goring of Colonel Jacinto Fierro by the bayonet in the hands of John Harned! And John Harned gored others with that bayonet. He was full of devils. He fought with many bullets in him, and he was hard to kill. And Maria Valenzuela was a brave woman. Unlike the other women, she did not cry out nor faint. She sat still in her box, gazing out across the bull-ring. Her face was white and she fanned herself, but she never looked around.

From all sides came the soldiers and officers and the common people bravely to subdue the mad Gringo. It is true—the cry went up from the crowd to kill all the Gringos. It is an old cry in Latin-American countries, what of the dislike for the Gringos and their uncouth ways. It is true, the cry went up. But the brave Ecuadorianos killed only John Harned, and first he killed seven of them. Besides, there were many hurt. I have seen many bull-fights, but never have I seen anything so abominable as the scene in the boxes when the fight was over. It was like a field of battle. The dead lay around everywhere, while the wounded sobbed and groaned and some of them died. One man, whom John Harned had thrust through the belly with the bayonet, clutched at himself with both his hands and screamed. I tell you for a fact it was more terrible than the screaming of a thousand horses.

No, Maria Valenzuela did not marry Luis Cervallos. I am sorry for that. He was my friend, and much of my money was invested in his ventures. It was five weeks before the surgeons took the bandages from his face. And there is a scar there to this day, on the cheek, under the eye. Yet John Harned struck him but once and struck him only with his naked fist. Maria Valenzuela is in Austria now. It is said she is to marry an Arch-Duke or some high nobleman. I do not know. I think she liked John Harned before he followed her to Quito to see the bull-fight. But why the horse? That is what I desire to know. Why should he watch the bull and say that it did not count, and then go immediately and most horribly mad because a horse screamed? There is no understanding the Gringos. They are barbarians.

WHEN THE WORLD WAS YOUNG

I

HE WAS A VERY QUIET, self-possessed sort of man, sitting a moment on top of the wall to sound the damp darkness for warnings of the dangers it might conceal. But the plummet of his hearing brought nothing to him save the moaning of wind through invisible trees and the rustling of leaves on swaying branches. A heavy fog drifted and drove before the wind, and though he could not see this fog, the wet of it blew upon his face, and the wall on which he sat was wet.

Without noise he had climbed to the top of the wall from the outside, and without noise he dropped to the ground on the inside. From his pocket he drew an electric night-stick, but he did not use it. Dark as the way was, he was not anxious for light. Carrying the night-stick in his hand, his finger on the button, he advanced through the darkness. The ground was velvety and springy to his feet, being carpeted with dead pine-needles and leaves and mold which evidently had been undisturbed for years. Leaves and branches brushed against his body, but so dark was it that he could not avoid them. Soon he walked with his hand stretched out gropingly before him, and more than once the hand fetched up against the solid trunks of massive trees. All about him he knew were these trees; he sensed the loom of them everywhere; and he experienced a strange feeling of microscopic smallness in the midst of great bulks leaning toward him to crush him. Beyond, he knew, was the house, and he expected to find some trail or winding path that would lead easily to it.

Once, he found himself trapped. On every side he groped against trees and branches, or blundered into thickets of underbrush, until there seemed no way out. Then he turned on his light, circumspectly, directing its rays to the ground at his feet. Slowly and carefully he moved it about him, the white brightness showing in sharp detail all the obstacles to his progress. He saw, an opening between huge-trunked trees, and advanced through it, putting out the light and treading on dry footing as yet protected from the drip of the fog by the dense foliage overhead. His sense of direction was good, and he knew he was going toward the house.

And then the thing happened—the thing unthinkable and unexpected. His descending foot came down upon something that was soft and alive, and that arose with a snort under the weight of his body. He sprang clear, and crouched for another spring, anywhere, tense and expectant, keyed for the onslaught of the unknown. He waited a moment, wondering what manner of animal it was that had arisen from under his foot and that now made no sound nor movement and that must be crouching and waiting just as tensely and expectantly as he. The strain became unbearable. Holding the night-stick before him, he pressed the button, saw, and screamed aloud in terror. He was prepared for anything, from a frightened calf or fawn to a belligerent lion, but he was not prepared for what he saw. In that instant his tiny searchlight, sharp and white, had shown him what a thousand years would not enable him to forget—a man, huge and blond, yellow-haired and yellow-bearded, naked except for soft-tanned moccasins and what seemed a goat-skin about his middle. Arms and legs were bare, as were his shoulders and most of his chest. The skin was smooth and hairless, but browned by sun and wind, while under it heavy muscles were knotted like fat snakes. Still, this alone, unexpected as it well was, was not what had made the man scream out. What had caused his terror was the unspeakable ferocity of the face, the wild-animal glare of the blue eyes scarcely dazzled by the light, the pine-needles matted and clinging in the beard and hair, and the whole formidable body crouched and in the act of springing at him. Practically in the instant he saw all this, and while his scream still rang, the thing leaped, he flung his night-stick full at it, and threw himself to the ground. He felt its feet and shins strike against his ribs, and he bounded up and away while the thing itself hurled onward in a heavy crashing fall into the underbrush.

As the noise of the fall ceased, the man stopped and on hands and knees waited. He could hear the thing moving about, searching for him, and he was afraid to advertise his location by attempting further flight. He knew that inevitably he would crackle the underbrush and be pursued. Once he drew out his revolver, then changed his mind. He had recovered his composure and hoped to get away without noise. Several times he heard the thing beating up the thickets for him, and there were moments when it, too, remained still and listened. This gave an idea to the man. One of his hands was resting on a chunk of dead wood. Carefully, first feeling about him in the darkness to know that the full swing of his arm was clear, he raised the chunk of wood and threw it. It was not a large piece, and it went far, landing noisily in a bush. He heard the thing bound into the bush, and at the same time himself crawled steadily away. And on hands and knees, slowly and cautiously, he crawled on, till his knees were wet on the soggy mold, When he listened he heard naught but the moaning wind and the drip-drip of the fog from the branches. Never abating his caution, he stood erect and went on to the stone wall, over which he climbed and dropped down to the road outside.

Feeling his way in a clump of bushes, he drew out a bicycle and prepared to mount. He was in the act of driving the gear around with his foot for the purpose of getting the opposite pedal in position, when he heard the thud of a heavy body that landed lightly and evidently on its feet. He did not wait for more, but ran, with hands on the handles of his bicycle, until he was able to vault astride the saddle, catch the pedals, and start a spurt. Behind he could hear the quick thud-thud of feet on the dust of the road, but he drew away from it and lost it. Unfortunately, he had started away from the direction of town and was heading higher up into the hills. He knew that on this particular road there were no cross roads. The only way back was past that terror, and he could not steel himself to face it. At the end of half an hour, finding himself on an ever increasing grade, he dismounted. For still greater safety, leaving the wheel by the roadside, he climbed through a fence into what he decided was a hillside pasture, spread a newspaper on the ground, and sat down.

"Gosh!" he said aloud, mopping the sweat and fog from his face.

And "Gosh!" he said once again, while rolling a cigarette and as he pondered the problem of getting back.

But he made no attempt to go back. He was resolved not to face that road in the dark, and with head bowed on knees, he dozed, waiting for daylight.

How long afterward he did not know, he was awakened by the yapping bark of a young coyote. As he looked about and located it on the brow of the hill behind him, he noted the change that had come over the face of the night. The fog was gone; the stars and moon were out; even the wind had died down. It had transformed into a balmy California summer night. He tried to doze again, but the yap of the coyote disturbed him. Half asleep, he heard a wild and eery chant. Looking about him, he noticed that the coyote had ceased its noise and was running away along the crest of the hill, and behind it, in full pursuit, no longer chanting, ran the naked creature he had encountered in the garden. It was a young coyote, and it was being overtaken when the chase passed from view. The man trembled as with a chill as he started to his feet, clambered over the fence, and mounted his wheel. But it was his chance and he knew it. The terror was no longer between him and Mill Valley.

He sped at a breakneck rate down the hill, but in the turn at the bottom, in the deep shadows, he encountered a chuck-hole and pitched headlong over the handle bar.

"It's sure not my night," he muttered, as he examined the broken fork of the machine.

Shouldering the useless wheel, he trudged on. In time he came to the stone wall, and, half disbelieving his experience, he sought in the road for tracks, and found them—moccasin tracks, large ones, deep-bitten into the dust at the toes. It was while bending over them, examining, that again he heard the eery chant. He had seen the thing pursue the coyote, and he knew he had no chance on a straight run. He did not attempt it, contenting himself with hiding in the shadows on the off side of the road.

And again he saw the thing that was like a naked man, running swiftly and lightly and singing as it ran. Opposite him it paused, and his heart stood still. But instead of coming toward his hiding-place, it leaped into the air, caught the branch of a roadside tree, and swung swiftly upward, from limb to limb, like an ape. It swung across the wall, and a dozen feet above the top, into the branches of another tree, and dropped out of sight to the ground. The man waited a few wondering minutes, then started on.

II

Dave Slotter leaned belligerently against the desk that barred the way to the private office of James Ward, senior partner of the firm of Ward, Knowles & Co. Dave was angry. Every one in the outer office had looked him over suspiciously, and the man who faced him was excessively suspicious.

"You just tell Mr. Ward it's important," he urged.

"I tell you he is dictating and cannot be disturbed," was the answer. "Come to-morrow."

"To-morrow will be too late. You just trot along and tell Mr. Ward it's a matter of life and death."

The secretary hesitated and Dave seized the advantage.

"You just tell him I was across the bay in Mill Valley last night, and that I want to put him wise to something."

"What name?" was the query.

"Never mind the name. He don't know me."

When Dave was shown into the private office, he was still in the belligerent frame of mind, but when he saw a large fair man whirl in a revolving chair from dictating to a stenographer to face him, Dave's demeanor abruptly changed. He did not know why it changed, and he was secretly angry with himself.

"You are Mr. Ward?" Dave asked with a fatuousness that still further irritated him. He had never intended it at all.

"Yes," came the answer.

"And who are you?"

"Harry Bancroft," Dave lied. "You don't know me, and my name don't matter."

"You sent in word that you were in Mill Valley last night?"

"You live there, don't you?" Dave countered, looking suspiciously at the stenographer.

"Yes. What do you mean to see me about? I am very busy."

"I'd like to see you alone, sir."

Mr. Ward gave him a quick, penetrating look, hesitated, then made up his mind.

"That will do for a few minutes, Miss Potter."

The girl arose, gathered her notes together, and passed out. Dave looked at Mr. James Ward wonderingly, until that gentleman broke his train of inchoate thought.

"Well?"

"I was over in Mill Valley last night," Dave began confusedly.

"I've heard that before. What do you want?"

And Dave proceeded in the face of a growing conviction that was unbelievable. "I was at your house, or in the grounds, I mean."

"What were you doing there?"

"I came to break in," Dave answered in all frankness.

"I heard you lived all alone with a Chinaman for cook, and it looked good to me. Only I didn't break in. Something happened that prevented. That's why I'm here. I come to warn you. I found a wild man loose in your grounds—a regular devil. He could pull a guy like me to pieces. He gave me the run of my life. He don't wear any clothes to speak of, he climbs trees like a monkey, and he runs like a deer. I saw him chasing a coyote, and the last I saw of it, by God, he was gaining on it."

Dave paused and looked for the effect that would follow his words. But no effect came. James Ward was quietly curious, and that was all.

"Very remarkable, very remarkable," he murmured. "A wild man, you say. Why have you come to tell me?"

"To warn you of your danger. I'm something of a hard proposition myself, but I don't believe in killing people. . . that is, unnecessarily. I realized that you was in danger. I thought I'd warn you. Honest, that's the game. Of course, if you wanted to give me anything for my trouble, I'd take it. That was in my mind, too. But I don't care whether you give me anything or not. I've warned you any way, and done my duty."

Mr. Ward meditated and drummed on the surface of his desk. Dave noticed they were large, powerful hands, withal well-cared for despite their dark sunburn. Also, he noted what had already caught his eye before—a tiny strip of flesh-colored courtplaster on the forehead over one eye. And still the thought that forced itself into his mind was unbelievable.

Mr. Ward took a wallet from his inside coat pocket, drew out a greenback, and passed it to Dave, who noted as he pocketed it that it was for twenty dollars.

"Thank you," said Mr. Ward, indicating that the interview was at an end.

"I shall have the matter investigated. A wild man running loose *is* dangerous."

But so quiet a man was Mr. Ward, that Dave's courage returned. Besides, a new theory had suggested itself. The wild man was evidently Mr. Ward's brother, a lunatic privately confined. Dave had heard of such things. Perhaps Mr. Ward wanted it kept quiet. That was why he had given him the twenty dollars.

"Say," Dave began, "now I come to think of it that wild man looked a lot like you—"

That was as far as Dave got, for at that moment he witnessed a transformation and found himself gazing into the same unspeakably ferocious blue eyes of the night before, at the same clutching talon-like hands, and at the same formidable bulk in the act of springing upon him. But this time Dave had no night-stick to throw, and he was caught by the biceps of both arms in a grip so terrific that it made him groan with pain. He saw the large white teeth exposed, for all the world as a dog's about to bite. Mr. Ward's beard brushed his face as the teeth went in for the grip on his throat. But the bite was not given. Instead, Dave felt the other's body stiffen as with an iron restraint, and then he was flung aside, without effort but with such force that only the wall stopped his momentum and dropped him gasping to the floor.

"What do you mean by coming here and trying to blackmail me?" Mr. Ward was snarling at him. "Here, give me back that money."

Dave passed the bill back without a word.

"I thought you came here with good intentions. I know you now. Let me see and hear no more of you, or I'll put you in prison where you belong. Do you understand?"

"Yes, sir," Dave gasped.

"Then go."

And Dave went, without further word, both his biceps aching intolerably from the bruise of that tremendous grip. As his hand rested on the door knob, he was stopped.

"You were lucky," Mr. Ward was saying, and Dave noted that his face and eyes were cruel and gloating and proud.

"You were lucky. Had I wanted, I could have torn your muscles out of your arms and thrown them in the waste basket there."

"Yes, sir," said Dave; and absolute conviction vibrated in his voice.

He opened the door and passed out. The secretary looked at him interrogatively.

"Gosh!" was all Dave vouchsafed, and with this utterance passed out of the offices and the story.

III

JAMES G. WARD WAS FORTY years of age, a successful business man, and very unhappy. For forty years he had vainly tried to solve a problem that was really himself and that with increasing years became more and more a woeful affliction. In himself he was two men, and, chronologically speaking, these men were several thousand years or so apart. He had studied the question of dual personality probably more profoundly than any half dozen of the leading specialists in that intricate and mysterious psychological field. In himself he was a different case from any that had been recorded. Even the most fanciful flights of the fiction-writers had not quite hit upon him. He was not a Dr. Jekyll and Mr. Hyde, nor was he like the unfortunate young man in Kipling's "Greatest Story in the World." His two personalities were so mixed that they were practically aware of themselves and of each other all the time.

His other self he had located as a savage and a barbarian living under the primitive conditions of several thousand years before. But which self was he, and which was the other, he could never tell. For he was both selves, and both selves all the time. Very rarely indeed did it happen that one self did not know what the other was doing. Another thing was that he had no visions nor memories of the past in which that early self had lived. That early self lived in the present; but while it lived in the present, it was under the compulsion to live the way of life that must have been in that distant past.

In his childhood he had been a problem to his father and mother, and to the family doctors, though never had they come within a thousand miles of hitting upon the clue to his erratic, conduct. Thus, they could not understand his excessive somnolence in the forenoon, nor his excessive activity at night. When they found him wandering along the hallways at night, or climbing over giddy roofs, or running in the hills, they decided he was a somnambulist. In reality he was wide-eyed awake and merely under the nightroaming compulsion of his early self. Questioned by an obtuse medico, he once told the truth and suffered the ignominy of having the revelation contemptuously labeled and dismissed as "dreams."

The point was, that as twilight and evening came on he became wakeful. The four walls of a room were an irk and a restraint. He heard a thousand voices whispering to him through the darkness. The night called to him, for he was, for that period of the twenty-four hours, essentially a night-prowler. But nobody understood, and never again did he attempt to explain. They classified him as a sleep-walker and took precautions accordingly—precautions that very often were futile. As his childhood advanced, he grew more cunning, so that the major portion of all his nights were spent in the open at realizing his other self. As a result, he slept in the forenoons. Morning studies and schools were impossible, and it was discovered that only in the afternoons, under private teachers, could he be taught anything. Thus was his modern self educated and developed.

But a problem, as a child, he ever remained. He was known as a little demon, of insensate cruelty and viciousness. The family medicos privately adjudged him a mental monstrosity and degenerate. Such few boy companions as he had, hailed him as a wonder, though they were all afraid of him. He could outclimb, outswim, outrun, outdevil any of them; while none dared fight with him. He was too terribly strong, madly furious.

When nine years of age he ran away to the hills, where he flourished, night-prowling, for seven weeks before he was discovered and brought home. The marvel was how he had managed to subsist and keep in condition during that time. They did not know, and he never told them, of the rabbits he had killed, of the quail, young and old, he had captured and devoured, of the farmers' chicken-roosts he had raided, nor of the cave-lair he had made and carpeted with dry leaves and grasses and in which he had slept in warmth and comfort through the forenoons of many days.

At college he was notorious for his sleepiness and stupidity during the morning lectures and for his brilliance in the afternoon. By collateral reading and by borrowing the notebook of his fellow students he managed to scrape through the detestable morning courses, while his afternoon courses were triumphs. In football he proved a giant and a terror, and, in almost every form of track athletics, save for strange Berserker rages that were sometimes displayed, he could be depended upon to win. But his fellows were afraid to box with him, and he signalized his last wrestling bout by sinking his teeth into the shoulder of his opponent.

After college, his father, in despair, sent him among the cow-punchers of a Wyoming ranch. Three months later the doughty cowmen confessed he was too much for them and telegraphed his father to come and take the wild man away. Also, when the father arrived to take him away, the cowmen allowed that they would vastly prefer chumming with howling cannibals, gibbering lunatics, cavorting gorillas, grizzly bears, and man-eating tigers than with this particular Young college product with hair parted in the middle.

There was one exception to the lack of memory of the life of his early self, and that was language. By some quirk of atavism, a certain portion of that early self's language had come down to him as a racial memory. In moments of happiness, exaltation, or battle, he was prone to burst out in wild barbaric songs or chants. It was by this means that he located in time and space that strayed half of him who should have been dead and dust for thousands of years. He sang, once, and deliberately, several of the ancient chants in the presence of Professor Wertz, who gave courses in old Saxon and who was a philogist of repute and passion. At the first one, the professor pricked up his ears and demanded to know what mongrel tongue or hog-German it was. When the second chant was rendered, the professor was highly excited. James Ward then concluded the performance by giving a song that always irresistibly rushed to his lips when he was engaged in fierce struggling or fighting. Then it was that Professor Wertz proclaimed it no hog-German, but early German, or early Teuton, of a date that must far precede anything that had ever been discovered and handed down by the scholars. So early was it that it was beyond him; yet it was filled with haunting reminiscences of word-forms he knew and which his trained intuition told him were true and real. He demanded the source of the songs, and asked to borrow the precious book that contained them. Also, he demanded to know why young Ward had always posed as being profoundly ignorant of the German language. And Ward could neither explain his ignorance nor lend the book. Whereupon, after pleadings and entreaties that extended through weeks, Professor Wert took a dislike to the young man, believed him a liar, and classified him as a man of monstrous selfishness for not giving him a glimpse of this wonderful screed that was older than the oldest any philologist had ever known or dreamed.

But little good did it do this much-mixed young man to know that half of him was late American and the other half early Teuton. Nevertheless, the late American in him was no weakling, and he (if he were a he and had a shred of existence outside of these two) compelled an adjustment or compromise between his one self that was a nightprowling savage that kept his other self sleepy of mornings, and that other self that was cultured and refined and that wanted to be normal and live and love and prosecute business like other people. The afternoons and early evenings he gave to the one, the nights to the other; the forenoons and parts of the nights were devoted to sleep for the twain. But in the mornings he slept in bed like a civilized man. In the night time he slept like a wild animal, as he had slept Dave Slotter stepped on him in the woods.

Persuading his father to advance the capital, he went into business and keen and successful business he made of it, devoting his afternoons whole-souled to it, while his partner devoted the mornings. The early evenings he spent socially, but, as the hour grew to nine or ten, an irresistible restlessness overcame him and he disappeared from the haunts of men until the next afternoon. Friends and acquaintances thought that he spent much of his time in sport. And they were right, though they never would have dreamed of the nature of the sport, even if they had seen him running coyotes in night-chases over the hills of Mill Valley. Neither were the schooner captains believed when they reported seeing, on cold winter mornings, a man swimming in the tide-rips of Raccoon Straits or in the swift currents between Goat island and Angel Island miles from shore.

In the bungalow at Mill Valley he lived alone, save for Lee Sing, the Chinese cook and factotum, who knew much about the strangeness of his master, who was paid well for saying nothing, and who never did say anything. After the satisfaction of his nights, a morning's sleep, and a breakfast of Lee Sing's, James Ward crossed the bay to San Francisco on a midday ferryboat and went to the club and on to his office, as normal and conventional a man of business as could be found in the city. But as the evening lengthened, the night called to him. There came a quickening of all his perceptions and a restlessness. His hearing was suddenly acute; the myriad night-noises told him a luring and familiar story; and, if alone, he would begin to pace up and down the narrow room like any caged animal from the wild.

Once, he ventured to fall in love. He never permitted himself that diversion again. He was afraid. And for many a day the young lady, scared at least out of a portion of her young ladyhood, bore on her arms and shoulders and wrists divers black-and-blue bruises—tokens of caresses which he had bestowed in all fond gentleness but too late at night. There was the mistake. Had he ventured love-making in the afternoon, all would have been well, for it would have been as the quiet gentleman that he would have made love—but at night it was the uncouth, wife-stealing savage of the dark German forests. Out of his wisdom, he decided that afternoon love-making could be prosecuted successfully; but out of the same wisdom he was convinced that marriage as would prove a ghastly failure. He found it appalling to imagine being married and encountering his wife after dark.

So he had eschewed all love-making, regulated his dual life, cleaned up a million in business, fought shy of match-making mamas and bright-eyed and eager young ladies of various ages, met Lilian Gersdale and made it a rigid observance never to see her later than eight o'clock in the evening, run of nights after his coyotes, and slept in forest lairs—and through it all had kept his secret safe save Lee Sing. . . and now, Dave Slotter. It was the latter's discovery of both his selves that frightened him. In spite of the counter fright he had given the burglar, the latter might talk. And even if he did not, sooner or later he would be found out by some one else.

Thus it was that James Ward made a fresh and heroic effort to control the Teutonic barbarian that was half of him. So well did he make it a point to see Lilian in the afternoons, that the time came when she accepted him for better or worse, and when he prayed privily and fervently that it was not for worse. During this period no prize-fighter ever trained more harshly and faithfully for a contest than he trained to subdue the wild savage in him. Among other things, he strove to exhaust himself during the day, so that sleep would render him deaf to the call of the night. He took a vacation from the office and went on long hunting trips, following the deer through the most inaccessible and rugged country he could find—and always in the daytime. Night found him indoors and tired. At home he installed a score of exercise machines, and where other men might go through a particular movement ten times, he went hundreds. Also, as a compromise, he built a sleeping porch on the second story. Here he at least breathed the blessed night air. Double screens prevented him from escaping into the woods, and each night Lee Sing locked him in and each morning let him out.

The time came, in the month of August, when he engaged additional servants to assist Lee Sing and dared a house party in his Mill Valley bungalow. Lilian, her mother and brother, and half a dozen mutual friends, were the guests. For two days and nights all went well. And on the third night, playing bridge till eleven o'clock, he had reason to be proud of himself. His restlessness fully hid, but as luck would have it, Lilian Gersdale was his opponent on his right. She was a frail delicate flower of a woman, and in his night-mood her very frailty incensed him. Not that he loved her less, but that he felt almost irresistibly impelled to reach out and paw and maul her. Especially was this true when she was engaged in playing a winning hand against him.

He had one of the deer-hounds brought in and, when it seemed he must fly to pieces with the tension, a caressing hand laid on the animal brought him relief. These contacts with the hairy coat gave him instant easement and enabled him to play out the evening. Nor did anyone guess the while terrible struggle their host was making, the while he laughed so carelessly and played so keenly and deliberately.

When they separated for the night, he saw to it that he parted from Lilian in the presence or the others. Once on his sleeping porch and safely locked in, he doubled and tripled and even quadrupled his exercises until, exhausted, he lay down on the couch to woo sleep and to ponder two problems that especially troubled him. One was this matter of exercise. It was a paradox. The more he exercised in this excessive fashion, the stronger he became. While it was true that he thus quite tired out his night-running Teutonic self, it seemed that he was merely setting back the fatal day when his strength would be too much for him and overpower him, and then it would be a strength more terrible than he had yet known. The other problem was that of his marriage and of the stratagems he must employ in order to avoid his wife after dark. And thus, fruitlessly pondering, he fell asleep.

Now, where the huge grizzly bear came from that night was long a mystery, while the people of the Springs Brothers' Circus, showing at Sausalito, searched long and vainly for "Big Ben, the Biggest Grizzly in Captivity." But Big Ben escaped, and, out of the mazes of half a thousand bungalows and country estates, selected the grounds of James J. Ward for visitation. The self first Mr. Ward knew was when he found him on his feet, quivering and tense, a surge of battle in his breast and on his lips the old war-chant. From without came a wild baying and bellowing of the hounds. And sharp as a knife-thrust through the pandemonium came the agony of a stricken dog—his dog, he knew.

Not stopping for slippers, pajama-clad, he burst through the door Lee Sing had so carefully locked, and sped down the stairs and out into the night. As his naked feet struck the graveled driveway, he stopped abruptly, reached under the steps to a hiding-place he knew well, and pulled forth a huge knotty club—his old companion on many a mad night adventure on the hills. The frantic hullabaloo of the dogs was coming nearer, and, swinging the club, he sprang straight into the thickets to meet it.

The aroused household assembled on the wide veranda. Somebody turned on the electric lights, but they could see nothing but one another's frightened faces. Beyond the brightly illuminated driveway the trees formed a wall of impenetrable blackness. Yet somewhere in that blackness a terrible struggle was going on. There was an infernal outcry of animals, a great snarling and growling, the sound of blows being struck and a smashing and crashing of underbrush by heavy bodies.

The tide of battle swept out from among the trees and upon the driveway just beneath the onlookers. Then they saw. Mrs. Gersdale cried out and clung fainting to her son. Lilian, clutching the railing so spasmodically that a bruising hurt was left in her finger-ends for days, gazed horror-stricken at a yellow-haired, wild-eyed giant whom she recognized as the man who was to be her husband. He was swinging a great club, and fighting furiously and calmly with a shaggy monster that was bigger than any bear she had ever seen. One rip of the beast's claws had dragged away Ward's pajama-coat and streaked his flesh with blood.

While most of Lilian Gersdale's fright was for the man beloved, there was a large portion of it due to the man himself. Never had she dreamed so formidable and magnificent a savage lurked under the starched shirt and conventional garb of her betrothed. And never had she had any conception of how a man battled. Such a battle was certainly not modern; nor was she there beholding a modern man, though she did not know it. For this was not Mr. James J. Ward, the San Francisco business man, but one, unnamed and unknown, a crude, rude savage creature who, by some freak of chance, lived again after thrice a thousand years.

The hounds, ever maintaining their mad uproar, circled about the fight, or dashed in and out, distracting the bear. When the animal turned to meet such flanking assaults, the man leaped in and the club came down. Angered afresh by every such blow, the bear would rush, and the man, leaping and skipping, avoiding the dogs, went backwards or circled to one side or the other. Whereupon the dogs, taking advantage of the opening, would again spring in and draw the animal's wrath to them.

The end came suddenly. Whirling, the grizzly caught a hound with a wide sweeping cuff that sent the brute, its ribs caved in and its back broken, hurtling twenty feet. Then the human brute went mad. A foaming rage flecked the lips that parted with a wild inarticulate cry, as it sprang in, swung the club mightily in both hands, and brought it down full on the head of the uprearing grizzly. Not even the skull of a grizzly could withstand the crushing force of such a blow, and the animal went down to meet the worrying of the hounds. And through their scurrying leaped the man, squarely upon the body, where, in the white electric light, resting on his club, he chanted a triumph in an unknown tongue—a song so ancient that Professor Wertz would have given ten years of his life for it.

His guests rushed to possess him and acclaim him, but James Ward, suddenly looking out of the eyes of the early Teuton, saw the fair frail Twentieth Century girl he loved, and felt something snap in his brain. He staggered weakly toward her, dropped the club, and nearly fell. Something had gone wrong with him. Inside his brain was an intolerable agony. It seemed as if the soul of him were flying asunder. Following the excited gaze of the others, he glanced back and saw the carcass of the bear. The sight filled him with fear. He uttered a cry and would have fled, had they not restrained him and led him into the bungalow.

JAMES J. WARD IS STILL at the head of the firm of Ward, Knowles & Co. But he no longer lives in the country; nor does he run of nights after the coyotes under the moon. The early Teuton in him died the night of the Mill Valley fight with the bear. James J. Ward is now wholly James J. Ward, and he shares no part of his being with any vagabond anachronism from the younger world. And so wholly is James J. Ward modern, that he knows in all its bitter fullness the curse of civilized fear. He is now afraid of the dark, and night in the forest is to him a thing of abysmal terror. His city house is of the spick and span order, and he evinces a great interest in burglarproof devices. His home is a tangle of electric wires, and after bed-time a guest can scarcely breathe without setting off an alarm. Also, he had invented a combination keyless door-lock that travelers may carry in their vest pockets and apply immediately and successfully under all circumstances. But his wife does not deem him a coward. She knows better. And, like any hero, he is content to rest on his laurels. His bravery is never questioned by those friends who are aware of the Mill Valley episode.

The Benefit of the Doubt

I

CARTER WATSON, A CURRENT MAGAZINE under his arm, strolled slowly along, gazing about him curiously. Twenty years had elapsed since he had been on this particular street, and the changes were great and stupefying. This Western city of three hundred thousand souls had contained but thirty thousand, when, as a boy, he had been wont to ramble along its streets. In those days the street he was now on had been a quiet residence street in the respectable workingclass quarter. On this late afternoon he found that it had been submerged by a vast and vicious tenderloin. Chinese and Japanese shops and dens abounded, all confusedly intermingled with low white resorts and boozing dens. This quiet street of his youth had become the toughest quarter of the city.

He looked at his watch. It was half-past five. It was the slack time of the day in such a region, as he well knew, yet he was curious to see. In all his score of years of wandering and studying social conditions over the world, he had carried with him the memory of his old town as a sweet and wholesome place. The metamorphosis he now beheld was startling. He certainly must continue his stroll and glimpse the infamy to which his town had descended.

Another thing: Carter Watson had a keen social and civic consciousness. Independently wealthy, he had been loath to dissipate his energies in the pink teas and freak dinners of society, while actresses, race-horses, and kindred diversions had left him cold. He had the ethical bee in his bonnet and was a reformer of no mean pretension, though his work had been mainly in the line of contributions to the heavier reviews and quarterlies and to the publication over his name of brightly, cleverly written books on the working classes and the slum-dwellers. Among the twenty-seven to his credit occurred titles such as, "If Christ Came to New Orleans," "The Worked-out Worker," "Tenement Reform in Berlin," "The Rural Slums of England," "The people of the East Side," "Reform Versus Revolution," "The University Settlement as a Hot Bed of Radicalism" and "The Cave Man of Civilization."

But Carter Watson was neither morbid nor fanatic. He did not lose his head over the horrors he encountered, studied, and exposed. No hair brained enthusiasm branded him. His humor saved him, as did his wide experience and his conservative philosophic temperament. Nor did he have any patience with lightning change reform theories. As he saw it, society would grow better only through the painfully slow and arduously painful processes of evolution. There were no short cuts, no sudden regenerations. The betterment of mankind must be worked out in agony and misery just as all past social betterments had been worked out.

But on this late summer afternoon, Carter Watson was curious. As he moved along he paused before a gaudy drinking place. The sign above read, "The Vendome." There were two entrances. One evidently led to the bar. This he did not explore. The other was a narrow hallway. Passing through this he found himself in a huge room, filled with chair-encircled tables and quite deserted. In the dim light he made out a piano in the distance. Making a mental note that he would come back some time and study the class of persons that must sit and drink at those multitudinous tables, he proceeded to circumnavigate the room.

Now, at the rear, a short hallway led off to a small kitchen, and here, at a table, alone, sat Patsy Horan, proprietor of the Vendome, consuming a hasty supper ere the evening rush of business. Also, Patsy Horan was angry with the world. He had got out of the wrong side of bed that morning, and nothing had gone right all day. Had his barkeepers been asked, they would have described his mental condition as a grouch. But Carter Watson did not know this. As he passed the little hallway, Patsy Horan's sullen eyes lighted on the magazine he carried under his arm. Patsy did not know Carter Watson, nor did he know that what he carried under his arm was a magazine. Patsy, out of the depths of his grouch, decided that this stranger was one of those pests who marred and scarred the walls of his back rooms by tacking up or pasting up advertisements. The color on the front cover of the magazine convinced him that it was such an advertisement. Thus the trouble began. Knife and fork in hand, Patsy leaped for Carter Watson.

"Out wid yeh!" Patsy bellowed. "I know yer game!"

Carter Watson was startled. The man had come upon him like the eruption of a jack-in-the-box.

"A defacin' me walls," cried Patsy, at the same time emitting a string of vivid and vile, rather than virile, epithets of opprobrium.

"If I have given any offense I did not mean to—"

But that was as far as the visitor got. Patsy interrupted.

"Get out wid yeh; yeh talk too much wid yer mouth," quoted Patsy, emphasizing his remarks with flourishes of the knife and fork.

Carter Watson caught a quick vision of that eating-fork inserted uncomfortably between his ribs, knew that it would be rash to talk further with his mouth, and promptly turned to go. The sight of his meekly retreating back must have further enraged Patsy Horan, for that worthy, dropping the table implements, sprang upon him.

Patsy weighed one hundred and eighty pounds. So did Watson. In this they were equal. But Patsy was a rushing, rough-and-tumble saloon-fighter, while Watson was a boxer. In this the latter had the advantage, for Patsy came in wide open, swinging his right in a perilous sweep. All Watson had to do was to straight-left him and escape. But Watson had another advantage. His boxing, and his experience in the slums and ghettos of the world, had taught him restraint.

He pivoted on his feet, and, instead of striking, ducked the other's swinging blow and went into a clinch. But Patsy, charging like a bull, had the momentum of his rush, while Watson, whirling to meet him, had no momentum. As a result, the pair of them went down, with all their three hundred and sixty pounds of weight, in a long crashing fall, Watson underneath. He lay with his head touching the rear wall of the large room. The street was a hundred and fifty feet away, and he did some quick thinking. His first thought was to avoid trouble. He had no wish to get into the papers of this, his childhood town, where many of his relatives and family friends still lived.

So it was that he locked his arms around the man on top of him, held him close, and waited for the help to come that must come in response to the crash of the fall. The help came—that is, six men ran in from the bar and formed about in a semi-circle.

"Take him off, fellows," Watson said. "I haven't struck him, and I don't want any fight."

But the semi-circle remained silent. Watson held on and waited. Patsy, after various vain efforts to inflict damage, made an overture.

"Leggo o' me an' I'll get off o' yeh," said he.

Watson let go, but when Patsy scrambled to his feet he stood over his recumbent foe, ready to strike.

"Get up," Patsy commanded.

His voice was stern and implacable, like the voice of God calling to judgment, and Watson knew there was no mercy there.

"Stand back and I'll get up," he countered.

"If yer a gentleman, get up," quoth Patsy, his pale blue eyes aflame with wrath, his fist ready for a crushing blow.

At the same moment he drew his foot back to kick the other in the face. Watson blocked the kick with his crossed arms and sprang to his feet so quickly that he was in a clinch with his antagonist before the latter could strike. Holding him, Watson spoke to the onlookers:

"Take him away from me, fellows. You see I am not striking him. I don't want to fight. I want to get out of here."

The circle did not move nor speak. Its silence was ominous and sent a chill to Watson's heart.

Patsy made an effort to throw him, which culminated in his putting Patsy on his back. Tearing loose from him, Watson sprang to his feet and made for the door. But the circle of men was interposed a wall. He noticed the white, pasty faces, the kind that never see the sun, and knew that the men who barred his way were the nightprowlers and preying beasts of the city jungle. By them he was thrust back upon the pursuing, bull-rushing Patsy.

Again it was a clinch, in which, in momentary safety, Watson appealed to the gang. And again his words fell on deaf ears. Then it was that he knew of many similar knew fear. For he had known of many similar situations, in low dens like this, when solitary men were man-handled, their ribs and features caved in, themselves beaten and kicked to death. And he knew, further, that if he were to escape he must neither strike his assailant nor any of the men who opposed him.

Yet in him was righteous indignation. Under no circumstances could seven to one be fair. Also, he was angry, and there stirred in him the fighting beast that is in all men. But he remembered his wife and children, his unfinished book, the ten thousand rolling acres of the up-country ranch he loved so well. He even saw in flashing visions the blue of the sky, the golden sun pouring down on his flower-spangled meadows, the lazy cattle knee-deep in the brooks, and the flash of trout in the riffles. Life was good-too good for him to risk it for a moment's sway of the beast. In short, Carter Watson was cool and scared.

His opponent, locked by his masterly clinch, was striving to throw him. Again Watson put him on the floor, broke away, and was thrust back by the pasty-faced circle to duck Patsy's swinging right and effect another clinch. This happened many times. And Watson grew even cooler, while the baffled Patsy, unable to inflict punishment, raged wildly and more wildly. He took to batting with his head in the clinches. The first time, he landed his forehead flush on Watson's nose. After that, the latter, in the clinches, buried his face in Patsy's breast. But the enraged Patsy batted on, striking his own eye and nose and cheek on the top of the other's head. The more he was thus injured, the more and the harder did Patsy bat.

This one-sided contest continued for twelve or fifteen minutes. Watson never struck a blow, and strove only to escape. Sometimes, in the free moments, circling about among the tables as he tried to win the door, the pasty-faced men gripped his coat-tails and flung him back at the swinging right of the on-rushing Patsy. Time upon time, and times without end, he clinched and put Patsy on his back, each time first whirling him around and putting him down in the direction of the door and gaining toward that goal by the length of the fall.

In the end, hatless, disheveled, with streaming nose and one eye closed, Watson won to the sidewalk and into the arms of a policeman.

"Arrest that man," Watson panted.

"Hello, Patsy," said the policeman. "What's the mix-up?"

"Hello, Charley," was the answer. "This guy comes in—"

"Arrest that man, officer," Watson repeated.

"G'wan! Beat it!" said Patsy.

"Beat it!" added the policeman. "If you don't, I'll pull you in."

"Not unless you arrest that man. He has committed a violent and unprovoked assault on me."

"Is it so, Patsy?" was the officer's query.

"Nah. Lemme tell you, Charley, an' I got the witnesses to prove it, so help me God. I was settin' in me kitchen eatin' a bowl of soup, when this guy comes in an' gets gay wid me. I never seen him in me born days before. He was drunk—"

"Look at me, officer," protested the indignant sociologist. "Am I drunk?"

The officer looked at him with sullen, menacing eyes and nodded to Patsy to continue.

"This guy gets gay wid me. 'I'm Tim McGrath,' says he, 'an' I can do the like to you,' says he. 'Put up yer hands.' I smiles, an' wid that, biff biff, he lands me twice an' spills me soup. Look at me eye. I'm fair murdered."

"What are you going to do, officer?" Watson demanded.

"Go on, beat it," was the answer, "or I'll pull you sure."

The civic righteousness of Carter Watson flamed up.

"Mr. Officer, I protest—"

But at that moment the policeman grabbed his arm with a savage jerk that nearly overthrew him.

"Come on, you're pulled."

"Arrest him, too," Watson demanded.

"Nix on that play," was the reply.

"What did you assault him for, him a peacefully eatin' his soup?"

II

Carter Watson was genuinely angry. Not only had he been wantonly assaulted, badly battered, and arrested, but the morning papers without exception came out with lurid accounts of his drunken brawl with the proprietor of the notorious Vendome. Not one accurate or truthful line was published. Patsy Horan and his satellites described the battle in detail. The one incontestable thing was that Carter Watson had been drunk. Thrice he had been thrown out of the place and into the gutter, and thrice he had come back, breathing blood and fire and announcing that he was going to clean out the place. "*Eminent Sociologist Jagged and Jugged*," was the first head-line he read, on the front page, accompanied by a large portrait of himself. Other headlines were: "*Carter Watson Aspired to Championship Honors*"; "*Carter Watson Gets His*"; "*Noted Sociologist Attempts to Clean Out a Tenderloin Café*"; and "*Carter Watson Knocked Out by Patsy Horan in Three Rounds*."

At the police court, next morning, under bail, appeared Carter Watson to answer the complaint of the People Versus Carter Watson, for the latter's assault and battery on one Patsy Horan. But first, the Prosecuting Attorney, who was paid to prosecute all offenders against the People, drew him aside and talked with him privately.

"Why not let it drop!" said the Prosecuting Attorney. "I tell you what you do, Mr. Watson: Shake hands with Mr. Horan and make it up, and we'll drop the case right here. A word to the Judge, and the case against you will be dismissed."

"But I don't want it dismissed," was the answer. "Your office being what it is, you should be prosecuting me instead of asking me to make up with this—this fellow."

"Oh, I'll prosecute you all right," retorted the Prosecuting Attorney.

"Also you will have to prosecute this Patsy Horan," Watson advised; "for I shall now have him arrested for assault and battery."

"You'd better shake and make up," the Prosecuting Attorney repeated, and this time there was almost a threat in his voice.

The trials of both men were set for a week later, on the same morning, in Police Judge Witberg's court.

"You have no chance," Watson was told by an old friend of his boyhood, the retired manager of the biggest paper in the city. "Everybody knows you were beaten up by this man. His reputation is most unsavory. But it won't help you in the least. Both cases will be dismissed. This will be because you are you. Any ordinary man would be convicted."

"But I do not understand," objected the perplexed sociologist. "Without warning I was attacked by this man; and badly beaten. I did not strike a blow. I—"

"That has nothing to do with it," the other cut him off.

"Then what is there that has anything to do with it?"

"I'll tell you. You are now up against the local police and political machine. Who are you? You are not even a legal resident in this town. You live up in the country. You haven't a vote of your own here. Much less do you swing any votes. This dive proprietor swings a string of votes in his precincts—a mighty long string."

"Do you mean to tell me that this Judge Witberg will violate the sacredness of his office and oath by letting this brute off?" Watson demanded.

"Watch him," was the grim reply. "Oh, he'll do it nicely enough. He will give an extra-legal, extra-judicial decision, abounding in every word in the dictionary that stands for fairness and right."

"But there are the newspapers," Watson cried.

"They are not fighting the administration at present. They'll give it to you hard. You see what they have already done to you."

"Then these snips of boys on the police detail won't write the truth?"

"They will write something so near like the truth that the public will believe it. They write their stories under instruction, you know. They have their orders to twist and color, and there won't be much left of you when they get done. Better drop the whole thing right now. You are in bad."

"But the trials are set."

"Give the word and they'll drop them now. A man can't fight a machine unless he has a machine behind him."

III

But Carter Watson was stubborn. He was convinced that the machine would beat him, but all his days he had sought social experience, and this was certainly something new.

The morning of the trial the Prosecuting Attorney made another attempt to patch up the affair.

"If you feel that way, I should like to get a lawyer to prosecute the case," said Watson.

"No, you don't," said the Prosecuting Attorney. "I am paid by the People to prosecute, and prosecute I will. But let me tell you. You have no chance. We shall lump both cases into one, and you watch out."

Judge Witberg looked good to Watson. A fairly young man, short, comfortably stout, smooth-shaven and with an intelligent face, he seemed a very nice man indeed. This good impression was added to by the smiling lips and the wrinkles of laughter in the corners of his black eyes. Looking at him and studying him, Watson felt almost sure that his old friend's prognostication was wrong.

But Watson was soon to learn. Patsy Horan and two of his satellites testified to a most colossal aggregation of perjuries. Watson could not have believed it possible without having experienced it. They denied the existence of the other four men. And of the two that testified, one claimed to have been in the kitchen, a witness to Watson's unprovoked assault on Patsy, while the other, remaining in the bar, had witnessed Watson's second and third rushes into the place as he attempted to annihilate the unoffending Patsy. The vile language ascribed to Watson was so voluminously and unspeakably vile, that he felt they were injuring their own case. It was so impossible that he should utter such things. But when they described the brutal blows he had rained on poor Patsy's face, and the chair he demolished when he vainly attempted to kick Patsy, Watson waxed secretly hilarious and at the same time sad. The trial was a farce, but such lowness of life was depressing to contemplate when he considered the long upward climb humanity must make.

Watson could not recognize himself, nor could his worst enemy have recognized him, in the swashbuckling, rough-housing picture that was painted of him. But, as in all cases of complicated perjury, rifts and contradictions in the various stories appeared. The Judge somehow failed to notice them, while the Prosecuting Attorney and Patsy's attorney shied off from them gracefully. Watson had not bothered to get a lawyer for himself, and he was now glad that he had not.

Still, he retained a semblance of faith in Judge Witberg when he went himself on the stand and started to tell his story.

"I was strolling casually along the street, your Honor," Watson began, but was interrupted by the Judge.

"We are not here to consider your previous actions," bellowed Judge Witberg. "Who struck the first blow?"

"Your Honor," Watson pleaded, "I have no witnesses of the actual fray, and the truth of my story can only be brought out by telling the story fully—"

Again he was interrupted.

"We do not care to publish any magazines here," Judge Witberg roared, looking at him so fiercely and malevolently that Watson could scarcely bring himself to believe that this was same man he had studied a few minutes previously.

"Who struck the first blow?" Patsy's attorney asked.

The Prosecuting Attorney interposed, demanding to know which of the two cases lumped together was, and by what right Patsy's lawyer, at that stage of the proceedings, should take the witness. Patsy's attorney fought back. Judge Witberg interfered, professing no knowledge of any two cases being lumped together. All this had to be explained. Battle royal raged, terminating in both attorneys apologizing to the Court and to each other. And so it went, and to Watson it had the seeming of a group of pickpockets ruffling and bustling an honest man as they took his purse. The machine was working, that was all.

"Why did you enter this place of unsavory reputations?" was asked him.

"It has been my custom for many years, as a student of economics and sociology, to acquaint myself—"

But this was as far as Watson got.

"We want none of your ologies here," snarled Judge Witberg. "It is a plain question. Answer it plainly. Is it true or not true that you were drunk? That is the gist of the question."

When Watson attempted to tell how Patsy had injured his face in his attempts to bat with his head, Watson was openly scouted and flouted, and Judge Witberg again took him in hand.

"Are you aware of the solemnity of the oath you took to testify to nothing but the truth on this witness stand?" the Judge demanded.

"This is a fairy story you are telling. It is not reasonable that a man would so injure himself, and continue to injure himself, by striking the soft and sensitive parts of his face against your head. You are a sensible man. It is unreasonable, is it not?"

"Men are unreasonable when they are angry," Watson answered meekly.

Then it was that Judge Witberg was deeply outraged and righteously wrathful.

"What right have you to say that?" he cried. "It is gratuitous. It has no bearing on the case. You are here as a witness, sir, of events that have transpired. The Court does not wish to hear any expressions of opinion from you at all."

"I but answered your question, your Honor," Watson protested humbly.

"You did nothing of the sort," was the next blast. "And let me warn you, sir, let me warn you, that you are laying yourself liable to contempt by such insolence. And I will have you know that we know how to observe the law and the rules of courtesy down here in this little courtroom. I am ashamed of you."

And, while the next punctilious legal wrangle between the attorneys interrupted his tale of what happened in the Vendome, Carter Watson, without bitterness, amused and at the same time sad, saw rise before him the machine, large and small, that dominated his country, the unpunished and shameless grafts of a thousand cities perpetrated by the spidery and vermin-like creatures of the machines. Here it was before him, a courtroom and a judge, bowed down in subservience by the machine to a dive-keeper who swung a string of votes. Petty and sordid as it was, it was one face of the many-faced machine that loomed colossally, in every city and state, in a thousand guises overshadowing the land.

A familiar phrase rang in his ears: "It is to laugh." At the height of the wrangle, he giggled, once, aloud, and earned a sullen frown from Judge Witberg. Worse, a myriad times, he decided, were these bullying lawyers and this bullying judge then the bucko mates in first quality hell-ships, who not only did their own bullying but protected themselves as well. These petty rapscallions, on the other hand, sought protection behind the majesty of the law. They struck, but no one was permitted to strike back, for behind them were the prison cells and the clubs of the stupid policemen—paid and professional fighters and beaters-up of men. Yet he was not bitter. The grossness and the sliminess of it was forgotten in the simple grotesqueness of it, and he had the saving sense of humor.

Nevertheless, hectored and heckled though he was, he managed in the end to give a simple, straightforward version of the affair, and, despite a belligerent cross-examination, his story was not shaken in any particular. Quite different it was from the perjuries that had shouted aloud from the perjuries of Patsy and his two witnesses.

Both Patsy's attorney and the Prosecuting Attorney rested their cases, letting everything go before the Court without argument. Watson protested against this, but was silenced when the Prosecuting Attorney told him that Public Prosecutor and knew his business.

"Patrick Horan has testified that he was in danger of his life and that he was compelled to defend himself," Judge Witberg's verdict began. "Mr. Watson has testified to the same thing. Each has sworn that the other struck the first blow; each has sworn that the other made an unprovoked assault on him. It is an axiom of the law that the defendant should be given the benefit of the doubt. A very reasonable doubt exists. Therefore, in the case of the People Versus Carter Watson the benefit of the doubt is given to said Carter Watson and he is herewith ordered discharged from custody. The same reasoning applies to the case of the People Versus Patrick Horan. He is given the benefit of the doubt and discharged from custody. My recommendation is that both defendants shake hands and make up."

In the afternoon papers the first headline that caught Watson's eye was: "*Carter Watson Acquitted.*" In the second paper it was: "*Carter Watson Escapes a Fine.*" But what capped everything was the one beginning: "*Carter Watson a Good Fellow.*" In the text he read how Judge Witberg had advised both fighters to shake hands, which they promptly did. Further, he read:

"'Let's have a nip on it,' said Patsy Horan.

"'Sure,' said Carter Watson.

"And, arm in arm, they ambled for the nearest saloon."

IV

Now, FROM THE WHOLE ADVENTURE, Watson carried away no bitterness. It was a social experience of a new order, and it led to the writing of another book, which he entitled, "*Police Court Procedure*: A Tentative Analysis."

One summer morning a year later, on his ranch, he left his horse and himself clambered on through a miniature canyon to inspect some rock ferns he had planted the previous winter. Emerging from the upper end of the canyon, he came out on one of his flower-spangled meadows, a delightful isolated spot, screened from the world by low hills and clumps of trees. And here he found a man, evidently on a stroll from the summer hotel down at the little town a mile away. They met face to face and the recognition was mutual. It was Judge Witberg. Also, it was a clear case of trespass, for Watson had trespass signs upon his boundaries, though he never enforced them.

Judge Witberg held out his hand, which Watson refused to see.

"Politics is a dirty trade, isn't it, Judge?" he remarked. "Oh, yes, I see your hand, but I don't care to take it. The papers said I shook hands with Patsy Horan after the trial. You know I did not, but let me tell you that I'd a thousand times rather shake hands with him and his vile following of curs, than with you."

Judge Witberg was painfully flustered, and as he hemmed and hawed and essayed to speak, Watson, looking at him, was struck by a sudden whim, and he determined on a grim and facetious antic.

"I should scarcely expect any animus from a man of your acquirements and knowledge of the world," the Judge was saying.

"Animus?" Watson replied. "Certainly not. I haven't such a thing in my nature. And to prove it, let me show you something curious, something you have never seen before." Casting about him, Watson picked up a rough stone the size of his fist. "See this. Watch me."

So saying, Carter Watson tapped himself a sharp blow on the cheek. The stone laid the flesh open to the bone and the blood spurted forth.

"The stone was too sharp," he announced to the astounded police judge, who thought he had gone mad.

"I must bruise it a trifle. There is nothing like being realistic in such matters."

Whereupon Carter Watson found a smooth stone and with it pounded his cheek nicely several times.

"Ah," he cooed. "That will turn beautifully green and black in a few hours. It will be most convincing."

"You are insane," Judge Witberg quavered.

"Don't use such vile language to me," said Watson. "You see my bruised and bleeding face? You did that, with that right hand of yours.

You hit me twice—biff, biff. It is a brutal and unprovoked assault. I am in danger of my life. I must protect myself."

Judge Witberg backed away in alarm before the menacing fists of the other.

"If you strike me I'll have you arrested," Judge Witberg threatened.

"That is what I told Patsy," was the answer. "And do you know what he did when I told him that?"

"No."

"That!"

And at the same moment Watson's right fist landed flush on Judge Witberg's nose, putting that legal gentleman over on his back on the grass.

"Get up!" commanded Watson. "If you are a gentleman, get up— that's what Patsy told me, you know."

Judge Witberg declined to rise, and was dragged to his feet by the coat-collar, only to have one eye blacked and be put on his back again. After that it was a red Indian massacre. Judge Witberg was humanely and scientifically beaten up. His checks were boxed, his cars cuffed, and his face was rubbed in the turf. And all the time Watson exposited the way Patsy Horan had done it. Occasionally, and very carefully, the facetious sociologist administered a real bruising blow. Once, dragging the poor Judge to his feet, he deliberately bumped his own nose on the gentleman's head. The nose promptly bled.

"See that!" cried Watson, stepping back and deftly shedding his blood all down his own shirt front. "You did it. With your fist you did it. It is awful. I am fair murdered. I must again defend myself."

And once more Judge Witberg impacted his features on a fist and was sent to grass.

"I will have you arrested," he sobbed as he lay.

"That's what Patsy said."

"A brutal—sniff, sniff,—and unprovoked—sniff, sniff—assault."

"That's what Patsy said."

"I will surely have you arrested."

"Speaking slangily, not if I can beat you to it."

And with that, Carter Watson departed down the canyon, mounted his horse, and rode to town.

An hour later, as Judge Witberg limped up the grounds to his hotel, he was arrested by a village constable on a charge of assault and battery preferred by Carter Watson.

V

"YOUR HONOR," WATSON SAID NEXT day to the village Justice, a well to do farmer and graduate, thirty years before, from a cow college, "since this Sol Witberg has seen fit to charge me with battery, following upon my charge of battery against him, I would suggest that both cases be lumped together. The testimony and the facts are the same in both cases."

To this the Justice agreed, and the double case proceeded. Watson, as prosecuting witness, first took the stand and told his story.

"I was picking flowers," he testified. "Picking flowers on my own land, never dreaming of danger. Suddenly this man rushed upon me from behind the trees. 'I am the Dodo,' he says, 'and I can do you to a frazzle. Put up your hands.' I smiled, but with that, biff, biff, he struck me, knocking me down and spilling my flowers. The language he used was frightful. It was an unprovoked and brutal assault. Look at my cheek. Look at my nose—I could not understand it. He must have been drunk. Before I recovered from my surprise he had administered this beating. I was in danger of my life and was compelled to defend himself. That is all, Your Honor, though I must say, in conclusion, that I cannot get over my perplexity. Why did he say he was the Dodo? Why did he so wantonly attack me?"

And thus was Sol Witberg given a liberal education in the art of perjury. Often, from his high seat, he had listened indulgently to police court perjuries in cooked-up cases; but for the first time perjury was directed against him, and he no longer sat above the court, with the bailiffs, the Policemen's clubs, and the prison cells behind him.

"Your Honor," he cried, "never have I heard such a pack of lies told by so bare-faced a liar—!"

Watson here sprang to his feet.

"Your Honor, I protest. It is for your Honor to decide truth or falsehood. The witness is on the stand to testify to actual events that have transpired. His personal opinion upon things in general, and upon me, has no bearing on the case whatever."

The Justice scratched his head and waxed phlegmatically indignant.

"The point is well taken," he decided. "I am surprised at you, Mr. Witberg, claiming to be a judge and skilled in the practice of the law, and yet being guilty of such unlawyerlike conduct. Your manner, sir, and your methods, remind me of a shyster. This is a simple case of assault and battery. We are here to determine who struck the first blow, and we are not interested in your estimates of Mr. Watson's personal character. Proceed with your story."

Sol Witberg would have bitten his bruised and swollen lip in chagrin, had it not hurt so much. But he contained himself and told a simple, straightforward, truthful story.

"Your Honor," Watson said, "I would suggest that you ask him what he was doing on my premises."

"A very good question. What were you doing, sir, on Mr. Watson's premises?"

"I did not know they were his premises."

"It was a trespass, your Honor," Watson cried. "The warnings are posted conspicuously."

"I saw no warnings," said Sol Witberg.

"I have seen them myself," snapped the Justice. "They are very conspicuous. And I would warn you, sir, that if you palter with the truth in such little matters you may darken your more important statements with suspicion. Why did you strike Mr. Watson?"

"Your Honor, as I have testified, I did not strike a blow."

The Justice looked at Carter Watson's bruised and swollen visage, and turned to glare at Sol Witberg.

"Look at that man's cheek!" he thundered. "If you did not strike a blow how comes it that he is so disfigured and injured?"

"As I testified—"

"Be careful," the Justice warned.

"I will be careful, sir. I will say nothing but the truth. He struck himself with a rock. He struck himself with two different rocks."

"Does it stand to reason that a man, any man not a lunatic, would so injure himself, and continue to injure himself, by striking the soft and sensitive parts of his face with a stone?" Carter Watson demanded

"It sounds like a fairy story," was the Justice's comment.

"Mr. Witberg, had you been drinking?"

"No, sir."

"Do you never drink?"

"On occasion."

The Justice meditated on this answer with an air of astute profundity.

Watson took advantage of the opportunity to wink at Sol Witberg, but that much-abused gentleman saw nothing humorous in the situation.

"A very peculiar case, a very peculiar case," the Justice announced, as he began his verdict. "The evidence of the two parties is flatly contradictory. There are no witnesses outside the two principals. Each claims the other committed the assault, and I have no legal way of determining the truth. But I have my private opinion, Mr. Witberg, and I would recommend that henceforth you keep off of Mr. Watson's premises and keep away from this section of the country—"

"This is an outrage!" Sol Witberg blurted out.

"Sit down, sir!" was the Justice's thundered command. "If you interrupt the Court in this manner again, I shall fine you for contempt. And I warn you I shall fine you heavily—you, a judge yourself, who should be conversant with the courtesy and dignity of courts. I shall now give my verdict:

"It is a rule of law that the defendant shall be given the benefit of the doubt. As I have said, and I repeat, there is no legal way for me to determine who struck the first blow. Therefore, and much to my regret,"—here he paused and glared at Sol Witberg—"in each of these cases I am compelled to give the defendant the benefit of the doubt. Gentlemen, you are both dismissed."

"Let us have a nip on it," Watson said to Witberg, as they left the courtroom; but that outraged person refused to lock arms and amble to the nearest saloon.

WINGED BLACKMAIL

P eter Winn lay back comfortably in a library chair, with closed eyes, deep in the cogitation of a scheme of campaign destined in the near future to make a certain coterie of hostile financiers sit up. The central idea had come to him the night before, and he was now reveling in the planning of the remoter, minor details. By obtaining control of a certain up-country bank, two general stores, and several logging camps, he could come into control of a certain dinky jerkwater line which shall here be nameless, but which, in his hands, would prove the key to a vastly larger situation involving more main-line mileage almost than there were spikes in the aforesaid dinky jerkwater. It was so simple that he had almost laughed aloud when it came to him. No wonder those astute and ancient enemies of his had passed it by.

The library door opened, and a slender, middle-aged man, weak-eyed and eye glassed, entered. In his hands was an envelope and an open letter. As Peter Winn's secretary it was his task to weed out, sort, and classify his employer's mail.

"This came in the morning post," he ventured apologetically and with the hint of a titter. "Of course it doesn't amount to anything, but I thought you would like to see it."

"Read it," Peter Winn commanded, without opening his eyes.

The secretary cleared his throat.

"It is dated July seventeenth, but is without address. Postmark San Francisco. It is also quite illiterate. The spelling is atrocious. Here it is:

"Mr. Peter Winn, *Sir*: I send you respectfully by express a pigeon worth good money. She's a loo-loo—"

"What is a loo-loo?" Peter Winn interrupted.

The secretary tittered.

"I'm sure I don't know, except that it must be a superlative of some sort. The letter continues:

"Please freight it with a couple of thousand-dollar bills and let it go. If you do I wont never annoy you no more. If you dont you will be sorry.

"That is all. It is unsigned. I thought it would amuse you."

"Has the pigeon come?" Peter Winn demanded.

"I'm sure I never thought to enquire."

"Then do so."

In five minutes the secretary was back.

"Yes, sir. It came this morning."

"Then bring it in."

The secretary was inclined to take the affair as a practical joke, but Peter Winn, after an examination of the pigeon, thought otherwise.

"Look at it," he said, stroking and handling it. "See the length of the body and that elongated neck. A proper carrier. I doubt if I've ever seen a finer specimen. Powerfully winged and muscled. As our unknown correspondent remarked, she is a loo-loo. It's a temptation to keep her."

The secretary tittered.

"Why not? Surely you will not let it go back to the writer of that letter."

Peter Winn shook his head.

"I'll answer. No man can threaten me, even anonymously or in foolery."

On a slip of paper he wrote the succinct message, "Go to hell," signed it, and placed it in the carrying apparatus with which the bird had been thoughtfully supplied.

"Now we'll let her loose. Where's my son? I'd like him to see the flight."

"He's down in the workshop. He slept there last night, and had his breakfast sent down this morning."

"He'll break his neck yet," Peter Winn remarked, half-fiercely, half-proudly, as he led the way to the veranda.

Standing at the head of the broad steps, he tossed the pretty creature outward and upward. She caught herself with a quick beat of wings, fluttered about undecidedly for a space, then rose in the air.

Again, high up, there seemed indecision; then, apparently getting her bearings, she headed east, over the oak-trees that dotted the park-like grounds.

"Beautiful, beautiful," Peter Winn murmured. "I almost wish I had her back."

But Peter Winn was a very busy man, with such large plans in his head and with so many reins in his hands that he quickly forgot the incident. Three nights later the left wing of his country house was blown up. It was not a heavy explosion, and nobody was hurt, though the wing itself was ruined. Most of the windows of the rest of the house were broken, and there was a deal of general damage. By the first ferry boat of the morning half a dozen San Francisco detectives arrived, and several hours later the secretary, in high excitement, erupted on Peter Winn.

"It's come!" the secretary gasped, the sweat beading his forehead and his eyes bulging behind their glasses.

"What has come?" Peter demanded. "It—the—the loo-loo bird."

Then the financier understood.

"Have you gone over the mail yet?"

"I was just going over it, sir."

"Then continue, and see if you can find another letter from our mysterious friend, the pigeon fancier."

The letter came to light. It read:

Mr. Peter Winn, *Honorable Sir*: Now dont be a fool. If youd came through, your shack would not have blew up—I beg to inform you respectfully, am sending same pigeon. Take good care of same, thank you. Put five one thousand dollar bills on her and let her go. Dont feed her. Dont try to follow bird. She is wise to the way now and makes better time. If you dont come through, watch out.

Peter Winn was genuinely angry. This time he indited no message for the pigeon to carry. Instead, he called in the detectives, and, under their advice, weighted the pigeon heavily with shot. Her previous flight having been eastward toward the bay, the fastest motor-boat in Tiburon was commissioned to take up the chase if it led out over the water.

But too much shot had been put on the carrier, and she was exhausted before the shore was reached. Then the mistake was made of putting too little shot on her, and she rose high in the air, got her bearings and started eastward across San Francisco Bay. She flew straight over Angel Island, and here the motor-boat lost her, for it had to go around the island.

That night, armed guards patrolled the grounds. But there was no explosion. Yet, in the early morning Peter Winn learned by telephone that his sister's home in Alameda had been burned to the ground.

Two days later the pigeon was back again, coming this time by freight in what had seemed a barrel of potatoes. Also came another letter:

Mr. Peter Winn, *Respectable Sir*: It was me that fixed yr sisters house. You have raised hell, aint you. Send ten thousand now. Going up all the time. Dont put any more handicap weights on that bird. You sure cant follow her, and its cruelty to animals.

Peter Winn was ready to acknowledge himself beaten. The detectives were powerless, and Peter did not know where next the man would strike—perhaps at the lives of those near and dear to him. He even telephoned to San Francisco for ten thousand dollars in bills of large denomination. But Peter had a son, Peter Winn, Junior, with the same firm-set jaw as his fathers, and the same knitted, brooding determination in his eyes. He was only twenty-six, but he was all man, a secret terror and delight to the financier, who alternated between pride in his son's aeroplane feats and fear for an untimely and terrible end.

"Hold on, father, don't send that money," said Peter Winn, Junior. "Number Eight is ready, and I know I've at last got that reefing down fine. It will work, and it will revolutionize flying. Speed—that's what's needed, and so are the large sustaining surfaces for getting started and for altitude. I've got them both. Once I'm up I reef down. There it is. The smaller the sustaining surface, the higher the speed. That was the law discovered by Langley. And I've applied it. I can rise when the air is calm and full of holes, and I can rise when its boiling, and by my control of my plane areas I can come pretty close to making any speed I want. Especially with that new Sangster-Endholm engine."

"You'll come pretty close to breaking your neck one of these days," was his father's encouraging remark.

"Dad, I'll tell you what I'll come pretty close to-ninety miles an hour—Yes, and a hundred. Now listen! I was going to make a trial tomorrow. But it won't take two hours to start today. I'll tackle it this afternoon. Keep that money. Give me the pigeon and I'll follow her to her loft where ever it is. Hold on, let me talk to the mechanics."

He called up the workshop, and in crisp, terse sentences gave his orders in a way that went to the older man's heart. Truly, his one son was a chip off the old block, and Peter Winn had no meek notions concerning the intrinsic value of said old block.

Timed to the minute, the young man, two hours later, was ready for the start. In a holster at his hip, for instant use, cocked and with the safety on, was a large-caliber automatic pistol. With a final inspection and overhauling he took his seat in the aeroplane. He started the engine, and with a wild burr of gas explosions the beautiful fabric darted down the launching ways and lifted into the air. Circling, as he rose, to the west, he wheeled about and jockeyed and maneuvered for the real start of the race.

This start depended on the pigeon. Peter Winn held it. Nor was it weighted with shot this time. Instead, half a yard of bright ribbon was firmly attached to its leg—this the more easily to enable its flight being followed. Peter Winn released it, and it arose easily enough despite the slight drag of the ribbon. There was no uncertainty about its movements. This was the third time it had made particular homing passage, and it knew the course.

At an altitude of several hundred feet it straightened out and went due east. The aeroplane swerved into a straight course from its last curve and followed. The race was on. Peter Winn, looking up, saw that the pigeon was outdistancing the machine. Then he saw something else. The aeroplane suddenly and instantly became smaller. It had reefed. Its high-speed plane-design was now revealed. Instead of the generous spread of surface with which it had taken the air, it was now a lean and hawklike monoplane balanced on long and exceedingly narrow wings.

WHEN YOUNG WINN REEFED DOWN so suddenly, he received a surprise. It was his first trial of the new device, and while he was prepared for increased speed he was not prepared for such an astonishing increase. It was better than he dreamed, and, before he knew it, he was hard upon the pigeon. That little creature, frightened by this, the most monstrous hawk it had ever seen, immediately darted upward, after the manner of pigeons that strive always to rise above a hawk.

In great curves the monoplane followed upward, higher and higher into the blue. It was difficult, from underneath to see the pigeon, and young Winn dared not lose it from his sight. He even shook out his reefs in order to rise more quickly. Up, up they went, until the pigeon, true to its instinct, dropped and struck at what it thought to be the back of its pursuing enemy. Once was enough, for, evidently finding no life in the smooth cloth surface of the machine, it ceased soaring and straightened out on its eastward course.

A carrier pigeon on a passage can achieve a high rate of speed, and Winn reefed again. And again, to his satisfaction, he found that he was beating the pigeon. But this time he quickly shook out a portion of his reefed sustaining surface and slowed down in time. From then on he knew he had the chase safely in hand, and from then on a chant rose to his lips which he continued to sing at intervals, and unconsciously, for the rest of the passage. It was: "Going some; going some; what did I tell you!—going some."

Even so, it was not all plain sailing. The air is an unstable medium at best, and quite without warning, at an acute angle, he entered an aerial tide which he recognized as the gulf stream of wind that poured through the drafty-mouthed Golden Gate. His right wing caught it first—a sudden, sharp puff that lifted and tilted the monoplane and threatened to capsize it. But he rode with a sensitive "loose curb," and quickly, but not too quickly, he shifted the angles of his wing-tips, depressed the front horizontal rudder, and swung over the rear vertical rudder to meet the tilting thrust of the wind. As the machine came back to an even keel, and he knew that he was now wholly in the invisible stream, he readjusted the wing-tips, rapidly away from him during the several moments of his discomfiture.

The pigeon drove straight on for the Alameda County shore, and it was near this shore that Winn had another experience. He fell into an air-hole. He had fallen into air-holes before, in previous flights, but this was a far larger one than he had ever encountered. With his eyes strained on the ribbon attached to the pigeon, by that fluttering bit of color he marked his fall. Down he went, at the pit of his stomach that old sink sensation which he had known as a boy he first negotiated quick-starting elevators. But Winn, among other secrets of aviation, had learned that to go up it was sometimes necessary first to go down. The air had refused to hold him. Instead of struggling futilely and perilously against this lack of sustension, he yielded to it. With steady head and hand, he depressed the forward horizontal rudder—just recklessly enough and not a fraction more—and the monoplane dived head foremost and sharply down the void. It was falling with the keenness of a knife-blade. Every instant the speed accelerated frightfully. Thus he accumulated the momentum that would save him. But few instants were required, when, abruptly shifting the double horizontal rudders forward and astern, he shot upward on the tense and straining plane and out of the pit.

At an altitude of five hundred feet, the pigeon drove on over the town of Berkeley and lifted its flight to the Contra Costa hills. Young Winn noted the campus and buildings of the University of California— his university—as he rose after the pigeon.

Once more, on these Contra Costa hills, he early came to grief. The pigeon was now flying low, and where a grove of eucalyptus presented a solid front to the wind, the bird was suddenly sent fluttering wildly upward for a distance of a hundred feet. Winn knew what it meant. It had been caught in an air-surf that beat upward hundreds of feet where the fresh west wind smote the upstanding wall of the grove. He reefed hastily to the uttermost, and at the same time depressed the angle of his flight to meet that upward surge. Nevertheless, the monoplane was tossed fully three hundred feet before the danger was left astern.

Two or more ranges of hills the pigeon crossed, and then Winn saw it dropping down to a landing where a small cabin stood in a hillside clearing. He blessed that clearing. Not only was it good for alighting, but, on account of the steepness of the slope, it was just the thing for rising again into the air.

A man, reading a newspaper, had just started up at the sight of the returning pigeon, when he heard the burr of Winn's engine and saw the huge monoplane, with all surfaces set, drop down upon him, stop suddenly on an air-cushion manufactured on the spur of the moment by a shift of the horizontal rudders, glide a few yards, strike ground, and come to rest not a score of feet away from him. But when he saw a young man, calmly sitting in the machine and leveling a pistol at him, the man turned to run. Before he could make the corner of the cabin, a bullet through the leg brought him down in a sprawling fall.

"What do you want!" he demanded sullenly, as the other stood over him.

"I want to take you for a ride in my new machine," Winn answered. "Believe me, she is a loo-loo."

The man did not argue long, for this strange visitor had most convincing ways. Under Winn's instructions, covered all the time by the pistol, the man improvised a tourniquet and applied it to his wounded leg. Winn helped him to a seat in the machine, then went to the pigeon-loft and took possession of the bird with the ribbon still fast to its leg.

A very tractable prisoner, the man proved. Once up in the air, he sat close, in an ecstasy of fear. An adept at winged blackmail, he had no aptitude for wings himself, and when he gazed down at the flying land and water far beneath him, he did not feel moved to attack his captor, now defenseless, both hands occupied with flight.

Instead, the only way the man felt moved was to sit closer.

Peter Winn, Senior, scanning the heavens with powerful glasses, saw the monoplane leap into view and grow large over the rugged backbone of Angel Island. Several minutes later he cried out to the waiting detectives that the machine carried a passenger. Dropping swiftly and piling up an abrupt air-cushion, the monoplane landed.

"That reefing device is a winner!" young Winn cried, as he climbed out. "Did you see me at the start? I almost ran over the pigeon. Going some, dad! Going some! What did I tell you? Going some!"

"But who is that with you?" his father demanded.

The young man looked back at his prisoner and remembered.

"Why, that's the pigeon-fancier," he said. "I guess the officers can take care of him."

Peter Winn gripped his son's hand in grim silence, and fondled the pigeon which his son had passed to him. Again he fondled the pretty creature. Then he spoke.

"Exhibit A, for the People," he said.

BUNCHES OF KNUCKLES

A rrangements quite extensive had been made for the celebration of Christmas on the yacht Samoset. Not having been in any civilized port for months, the stock of provisions boasted few delicacies; yet Minnie Duncan had managed to devise real feasts for cabin and forecastle.

"Listen, Boyd," she told her husband. "Here are the menus. For the cabin, raw bonita native style, turtle soup, omelette a la Samoset—"

"What the dickens?" Boyd Duncan interrupted.

"Well, if you must know, I found a tin of mushrooms and a package of egg-powder which had fallen down behind the locker, and there are other things as well that will go into it. But don't interrupt. Boiled yam, fried taro, alligator pear salad—there, you've got me all mixed, Then I found a last delectable half-pound of dried squid. There will be baked beans Mexican, if I can hammer it into Toyama's head; also, baked papaia with Marquesan honey, and, lastly, a wonderful pie the secret of which Toyama refuses to divulge."

"I wonder if it is possible to concoct a punch or a cocktail out of trade rum?" Duncan muttered gloomily.

"Oh! I forgot! Come with me."

His wife caught his hand and led him through the small connecting door to her tiny stateroom. Still holding his hand, she fished in the depths of a hat-locker and brought forth a pint bottle of champagne.

"The dinner is complete!" he cried.

"Wait."

She fished again, and was rewarded with a silver-mounted whisky flask. She held it to the light of a port-hole, and the liquor showed a quarter of the distance from the bottom.

"I've been saving it for weeks," she explained. "And there's enough for you and Captain Dettmar."

"Two mighty small drinks," Duncan complained.

"There would have been more, but I gave a drink to Lorenzo when he was sick."

Duncan growled, "Might have given him rum," facetiously.

"The nasty stuff! For a sick man? Don't be greedy, Boyd. And I'm glad there isn't any more, for Captain Dettmar's sake. Drinking always makes him irritable. And now for the men's dinner. Soda crackers, sweet cakes, candy—"

"Substantial, I must say."

"Do hush. Rice, and curry, yam, taro, bonita, of course, a big cake Toyama is making, young pig—"

"Oh, I say," he protested.

"It is all right, Boyd. We'll be in Attu-Attu in three days. Besides, it's my pig. That old chief what-ever-his-name distinctly presented it to me. You saw him yourself. And then two tins of bullamacow. That's their dinner. And now about the presents. Shall we wait until tomorrow, or give them this evening?"

"Christmas Eve, by all means," was the man's judgment. "We'll call all hands at eight bells; I'll give them a tot of rum all around, and then you give the presents. Come on up on deck. It's stifling down here. I hope Lorenzo has better luck with the dynamo; without the fans there won't be much sleeping to-night if we're driven below."

They passed through the small main-cabin, climbed a steep companion ladder, and emerged on deck. The sun was setting, and the promise was for a clear tropic night. The Samoset, with fore- and main-sail winged out on either side, was slipping a lazy four-knots through the smooth sea. Through the engine-room skylight came a sound of hammering. They strolled aft to where Captain Dettmar, one foot on the rail, was oiling the gear of the patent log. At the wheel stood a tall South Sea Islander, clad in white undershirt and scarlet hip-cloth.

Boyd Duncan was an original. At least that was the belief of his friends. Of comfortable fortune, with no need to do anything but take his comfort, he elected to travel about the world in outlandish and most uncomfortable ways. Incidentally, he had ideas about coral-reefs, disagreed profoundly with Darwin on that subject, had voiced his opinion in several monographs and one book, and was now back at his hobby, cruising the South Seas in a tiny, thirty-ton yacht and studying reef-formations.

His wife, Minnie Duncan, was also declared an original, inasmuch as she joyfully shared his vagabond wanderings. Among other things, in the six exciting years of their marriage she had climbed Chimborazo with him, made a three-thousand-mile winter journey with dogs and sleds in Alaska, ridden a horse from Canada to Mexico, cruised the Mediterranean in a ten-ton yawl, and canoed from Germany to the Black Sea across the heart of Europe. They were a royal pair of wanderlusters, he, big and broad-shouldered, she a small, brunette, and happy woman, whose one hundred and fifteen pounds were all grit and endurance, and withal, pleasing to look upon.

The Samoset had been a trading schooner, when Duncan bought her in San Francisco and made alterations. Her interior was wholly rebuilt, so that the hold became main-cabin and staterooms, while abaft amidships were installed engines, a dynamo, an ice machine, storage batteries, and, far in the stern, gasoline tanks. Necessarily, she carried a small crew. Boyd, Minnie, and Captain Dettmar were the only whites on board, though Lorenzo, the small and greasy engineer, laid a part claim to white, being a Portuguese half-caste. A Japanese served as cook, and a Chinese as cabin boy. Four white sailors had constituted the original crew for'ard, but one by one they had yielded to the charms of palm-waving South Sea isles and been replaced by islanders. Thus, one of the dusky sailors hailed from Easter Island, a second from the Carolines, a third from the Paumotus, while the fourth was a gigantic Samoan. At sea, Boyd Duncan, himself a navigator, stood a mate's watch with Captain Dettmar, and both of them took a wheel or lookout occasionally. On a pinch, Minnie herself could take a wheel, and it was on pinches that she proved herself more dependable at steering than did the native sailors.

At eight bells, all hands assembled at the wheel, and Boyd Duncan appeared with a black bottle and a mug. The rum he served out himself, half a mug of it to each man. They gulped the stuff down with many facial expressions of delight, followed by loud lip-smackings of approval, though the liquor was raw enough and corrosive enough to burn their mucous membranes. All drank except Lee Goom, the abstemious cabin boy. This rite accomplished, they waited for the next, the present-giving. Generously molded on Polynesian lines, huge-bodied and heavy-muscled, they were nevertheless like so many children, laughing merrily at little things, their eager black eyes flashing in the lantern light as their big bodies swayed to the heave and roll of the ship.

Calling each by name, Minnie gave the presents out, accompanying each presentation with some happy remark that added to the glee. There were trade watches, clasp knives, amazing assortments of fish-hooks in packages, plug tobacco, matches, and gorgeous strips of cotton for loincloths all around. That Boyd Duncan was liked by them was evidenced by the roars of laughter with which they greeted his slightest joking allusion.

Captain Dettmar, white-faced, smiling only when his employer chanced to glance at him, leaned against the wheel-box, looking on. Twice, he left the group and went below, remaining there but a minute each time. Later, in the main cabin, when Lorenzo, Lee Goom and Toyama received their presents, he disappeared into his stateroom twice again. For of all times, the devil that slumbered in Captain Dettmar's soul chose this particular time of good cheer to awaken. Perhaps it was not entirely the devil's fault, for Captain Dettmar, privily cherishing a quart of whisky for many weeks, had selected Christmas Eve for broaching it.

It was still early in the evening—two bells had just gone—when Duncan and his wife stood by the cabin companionway, gazing to windward and canvassing the possibility of spreading their beds on deck. A small, dark blot of cloud, slowly forming on the horizon, carried the threat of a rain-squall, and it was this they were discussing when Captain Dettmar, coming from aft and about to go below, glanced at them with sudden suspicion. He paused, his face working spasmodically. Then he spoke:

"You are talking about me."

His voice was hoarse, and there was an excited vibration in it. Minnie Duncan started, then glanced at her husband's immobile face, took the cue, and remained silent.

"I say you were talking about me," Captain Dettmar repeated, this time with almost a snarl.

He did not lurch nor betray the liquor on him in any way save by the convulsive working of his face.

"Minnie, you'd better go down," Duncan said gently. "Tell Lee Goom we'll sleep below. It won't be long before that squall is drenching things."

She took the hint and left, delaying just long enough to give one anxious glance at the dim faces of the two men.

Duncan puffed at his cigar and waited till his wife's voice, in talk with the cabin-boy, came up through the open skylight.

"Well?" Duncan demanded in a low voice, but sharply.

"I said you were talking about me. I say it again. Oh, I haven't been blind. Day after day I've seen the two of you talking about me. Why don't you come out and say it to my face! I know you know. And I know your mind's made up to discharge me at Attu-Attu."

"I am sorry you are making such a mess of everything," was Duncan's quiet reply.

But Captain Dettmar's mind was set on trouble.

"You know you are going to discharge me. You think you are too good to associate with the likes of me—you and your wife."

"Kindly keep her out of this," Duncan warned. "What do you want?"

"I want to know what you are going to do!"

"Discharge you, after this, at Attu-Attu."

"You intended to, all along."

"On the contrary. It is your present conduct that compels me."

"You can't give me that sort of talk."

"I can't retain a captain who calls me a liar."

Captain Dettmar for the moment was taken aback. His face and lips worked, but he could say nothing. Duncan coolly pulled at his cigar and glanced aft at the rising cloud of squall.

"Lee Goom brought the mail aboard at Tahiti," Captain Dettmar began.

"We were hove short then and leaving. You didn't look at your letters until we were outside, and then it was too late. That's why you didn't discharge me at Tahiti. Oh, I know. I saw the long envelope when Lee Goom came over the side. It was from the Governor of California, printed on the corner for any one to see. You'd been working behind my back. Some beachcomber in Honolulu had whispered to you, and you'd written to the Governor to find out. And that was his answer Lee Goom carried out to you. Why didn't you come to me like a man! No, you must play underhand with me, knowing that this billet was the one chance for me to get on my feet again. And as soon as you read the Governor's letter your mind was made up to get rid of me. I've seen it on your face ever since for all these months.. I've seen the two of you, polite as hell to me all the time, and getting away in corners and talking about me and that affair in 'Frisco."

"Are you done?" Duncan asked, his voice low, and tense. "Quite done?"

Captain Dettmar made no answer.

"Then I'll tell you a few things. It was precisely because of that affair in 'Frisco that I did not discharge you in Tahiti. God knows you gave me sufficient provocation. I thought that if ever a man needed a chance to rehabilitate himself, you were that man. Had there been no black mark against you, I would have discharged you when I learned how you were robbing me."

Captain Dettmar showed surprise, started to interrupt, then changed his mind.

"There was that matter of the deck-calking, the bronze rudder-irons, the overhauling of the engine, the new spinnaker boom, the new davits, and the repairs to the whale-boat. You OKd the shipyard bill. It was four thousand one hundred and twenty-two francs. By the regular shipyard charges it ought not to have been a centime over twenty-five hundred francs-"

"If you take the word of those alongshore sharks against mine—" the other began thickly.

"Save yourself the trouble of further lying," Duncan went on coldly. "I looked it up. I got Flaubin before the Governor himself, and the old rascal confessed to sixteen hundred overcharge. Said you'd stuck him up for it. Twelve hundred went to you, and his share was four hundred and the job. Don't interrupt. I've got his affidavit below. Then was when I would have put you ashore, except for the cloud you were under. You had to have this one chance or go clean to hell. I gave you the chance. And what have you got to say about it?"

"What did the Governor say?" Captain Dettmar demanded truculently.

"Which governor?"

"Of California. Did he lie to you like all the rest?"

"I'll tell you what he said. He said that you had been convicted on circumstantial evidence; that was why you had got life imprisonment instead of hanging; that you had always stoutly maintained your innocence; that you were the black sheep of the Maryland Dettmars; that they moved heaven and earth for your pardon; that your prison conduct was most exemplary; that he was prosecuting attorney at the time you were convicted; that after you had served seven years he yielded to your family's plea and pardoned you; and that in his own mind existed a doubt that you had killed McSweeny."

There was a pause, during which Duncan went on studying the rising squall, while Captain Dettmar's face worked terribly.

"Well, the Governor was wrong," he announced, with a short laugh. "I did kill McSweeny. I did get the watchman drunk that night. I beat McSweeny to death in his bunk. I used the iron belaying pin that appeared in the evidence. He never had a chance. I beat him to a jelly. Do you want the details?"

Duncan looked at him in the curious way one looks at any monstrosity, but made no reply.

"Oh, I'm not afraid to tell you," Captain Dettmar blustered on. "There are no witnesses. Besides, I am a free man now. I am pardoned, and by God they can never put me back in that hole again. I broke

McSweeny's jaw with the first blow. He was lying on his back asleep. He said, 'My God, Jim! My God!' It was funny to see his broken jaw wabble as he said it. Then I smashed him. . . I say, do you want the rest of the details?"

"Is that all you have to say?" was the answer.

"Isn't it enough?" Captain Dettmar retorted.

"It is enough."

"What are you going to do about it?"

"Put you ashore at Attu-Attu."

"And in the meantime?"

"In the meantime. . ." Duncan paused. An increase of weight in the wind rippled his hair. The stars overhead vanished, and the Samoset swung four points off her course in the careless steersman's hands. "In the meantime throw your halyards down on deck and look to your wheel. I'll call the men."

The next moment the squall burst upon them. Captain Dettmar, springing aft, lifted the coiled mainsail halyards from their pins and threw them, ready to run, on the deck. The three islanders swarmed from the tiny forecastle, two of them leaping to the halyards and holding by a single turn, while the third fastened down the engineroom, companion and swung the ventilators around. Below, Lee Goom and Toyama were lowering skylight covers and screwing up deadeyes. Duncan pulled shut the cover of the companion scuttle, and held on, waiting, the first drops of rain pelting his face, while the Samoset leaped violently ahead, at the same time heeling first to starboard then to port as the gusty pressures caught her winged-out sails.

All waited. But there was no need to lower away on the run. The power went out of the wind, and the tropic rain poured a deluge over everything. Then it was, the danger past, and as the Kanakas began to coil the halyards back on the pins, that Boyd Duncan went below.

"All right," he called in cheerily to his wife. "Only a puff."

"And Captain Dettmar?" she queried.

"Has been drinking, that is all. I shall get rid of him at Attu-Attu."

But before Duncan climbed into his bunk, he strapped around himself, against the skin and under his pajama coat, a heavy automatic pistol.

He fell asleep almost immediately, for his was the gift of perfect relaxation. He did things tensely, in the way savages do, but the instant the need passed he relaxed, mind and body. So it was that he slept, while the rain still poured on deck and the yacht plunged and rolled in the brief, sharp sea caused by the squall.

He awoke with a feeling of suffocation and heaviness. The electric fans had stopped, and the air was thick and stifling. Mentally cursing all Lorenzos and storage batteries, he heard his wife moving in the adjoining stateroom and pass out into the main cabin. Evidently heading for the fresher air on deck, he thought, and decided it was a good example to imitate. Putting on his slippers and tucking a pillow and a blanket under his arm, he followed her. As he was about to emerge from the companionway, the ship's clock in the cabin began to strike and he stopped to listen. Four bells sounded. It was two in the morning. From without came the creaking of the gaff-jaw against the mast. The Samoset rolled and righted on a sea, and in the light breeze her canvas gave forth a hollow thrum.

He was just putting his foot out on the damp deck when he heard his wife scream. It was a startled frightened scream that ended in a splash overside. He leaped out and ran aft. In the dim starlight he could make out her head and shoulders disappearing astern in the lazy wake.

"What was it?" Captain Dettmar, who was at the wheel, asked.

"Mrs. Duncan," was Duncan's reply, as he tore the life-buoy from its hook and flung it aft. "Jibe over to starboard and come up on the wind!" he commanded.

And then Boyd Duncan made a mistake. He dived overboard.

When he came up, he glimpsed the blue-light on the buoy, which had ignited automatically when it struck the water. He swam for it, and found Minnie had reached it first.

"Hello," he said. "Just trying to keep cool?"

"Oh, Boyd!" was her answer, and one wet hand reached out and touched his.

The blue light, through deterioration or damage, flickered out. As they lifted on the smooth crest of a wave, Duncan turned to look where the Samoset made a vague blur in the darkness. No lights showed, but there was noise of confusion. He could hear Captain Dettmar's shouting above the cries of the others.

"I must say he's taking his time," Duncan grumbled. "Why doesn't he jibe? There she goes now."

They could hear the rattle of the boom tackle blocks as the sail was eased across.

"That was the mainsail," he muttered. "Jibed to port when I told him starboard."

Again they lifted on a wave, and again and again, ere they could make out the distant green of the Samoset's starboard light. But instead of remaining stationary, in token that the yacht was coming toward them, it began moving across their field of vision. Duncan swore.

"What's the lubber holding over there for!" he demanded. "He's got his compass. He knows our bearing."

But the green light, which was all they could see, and which they could see only when they were on top of a wave, moved steadily away from them, withal it was working up to windward, and grew dim and dimmer. Duncan called out loudly and repeatedly, and each time, in the intervals, they could hear, very faintly, the voice of Captain Dettmar shouting orders.

"How can he hear me with such a racket?" Duncan complained.

"He's doing it so the crew won't hear you," was Minnie's answer.

There was something in the quiet way she said it that caught her husband's attention.

"What do you mean?"

"I mean that he is not trying to pick us up," she went on in the same composed voice. "He threw me overboard."

"You are not making a mistake?"

"How could I? I was at the main rigging, looking to see if any more rain threatened. He must have left the wheel and crept behind me. I was holding on to a stay with one hand. He gripped my hand free from behind and threw me over. It's too bad you didn't know, or else you would have staid aboard."

Duncan groaned, but said nothing for several minutes. The green light changed the direction of its course.

"She's gone about," he announced. "You are right. He's deliberately working around us and to windward. Up wind they can never hear me. But here goes."

He called at minute intervals for a long time. The green light disappeared, being replaced by the red, showing that the yacht had gone about again.

"Minnie," he said finally, "it pains me to tell you, but you married a fool. Only a fool would have gone overboard as I did."

"What chance have we of being picked up. . . by some other vessel, I mean?" she asked.

"About one in ten thousand, or ten thousand million. Not a steamer route nor trade route crosses this stretch of ocean. And there aren't any whalers knocking about the South Seas. There might be a stray trading schooner running across from Tutuwanga. But I happen to know that island is visited only once a year. A chance in a million is ours."

"And we'll play that chance," she rejoined stoutly.

"You *are* a joy!" His hand lifted hers to his lips. "And Aunt Elizabeth always wondered what I saw in you. Of course we'll play that chance. And we'll win it, too. To happen otherwise would be unthinkable. Here goes."

He slipped the heavy pistol from his belt and let it sink into the sea. The belt, however, he retained.

"Now you get inside the buoy and get some sleep. Duck under."

She ducked obediently, and came up inside the floating circle. He fastened the straps for her, then, with the pistol belt, buckled himself across one shoulder to the outside of the buoy.

"We're good for all day to-morrow," he said. "Thank God the water's warm. It won't be a hardship for the first twenty-hour hours, anyway. And if we're not picked up by nightfall, we've just got to hang on for another day, that's all."

For half an hour they maintained silence, Duncan, his head resting on the arm that was on the buoy, seemed asleep.

"Boyd?" Minnie said softly.

"Thought you were asleep," he growled.

"Boyd, if we don't come through this—"

"Stow that!" he broke in ungallantly. "Of course we're coming through. There is isn't a doubt of it. Somewhere on this ocean is a ship that's heading right for us. You wait and see. Just the same I wish my brain were equipped with wireless. Now I'm going to sleep, if you don't."

But for once, sleep baffled him. An hour later he heard Minnie stir and knew she was awake.

"Say, do you know what I've been thinking!" she asked.

"No; what?"

"That I'll wish you a Merry Christmas."

"By George, I never thought of it. Of course it's Christmas Day. We'll have many more of them, too. And do you know what I've been thinking? What a confounded shame we're done out of our Christmas dinner. Wait till I lay hands on Dettmar. I'll take it out of him. And it won't be with an iron belaying pin either, Just two bunches of naked knuckles, that's all."

Despite his facetiousness, Boyd Duncan had little hope. He knew well enough the meaning of one chance in a million, and was calmly certain that his wife and he had entered upon their last few living hours—hours that were inevitably bound to be black and terrible with tragedy.

The tropic sun rose in a cloudless sky. Nothing was to be seen. The Samoset was beyond the sea-rim. As the sun rose higher, Duncan ripped his pajama trousers in halves and fashioned them into two rude turbans. Soaked in sea-water they offset the heat-rays.

"When I think of that dinner, I'm really angry," he complained, as he noted an anxious expression threatening to set on his wife's face. "And I want you to be with me when I settle with Dettmar. I've always been opposed to women witnessing scenes of blood, but this is different. It will be a beating."

"I hope I don't break my knuckles on him," he added, after a pause.

Midday came and went, and they floated on, the center of a narrow sea-circle. A gentle breath of the dying trade-wind fanned them, and they rose and fell monotonously on the smooth swells of a perfect summer sea. Once, a gunie spied them, and for half an hour circled about them with majestic sweeps. And, once, a huge rayfish, measuring a score of feet across the tips, passed within a few yards.

By sunset, Minnie began to rave, softly, babblingly, like a child. Duncan's face grew haggard as he watched and listened, while in his mind he revolved plans of how best to end the hours of agony that were coming. And, so planning, as they rose on a larger swell than usual, he swept the circle of the sea with his eyes, and saw, what made him cry out.

"Minnie!" She did not answer, and he shouted her name again in her ear, with all the voice he could command. Her eyes opened, in them fluttered commingled consciousness and delirium. He slapped her hands and wrists till the sting of the blows roused her.

"There she is, the chance in a million!" he cried.

"A steamer at that, heading straight for us! By George, it's a cruiser! I have it!—the Annapolis, returning with those astronomers from Tutuwanga."

United States Consul Lingford was a fussy, elderly gentleman, and in the two years of his service at Attu-Attu had never encountered so unprecedented a case as that laid before him by Boyd Duncan. The latter, with his wife, had been landed there by the Annapolis, which had promptly gone on with its cargo of astronomers to Fiji.

"It was cold-blooded, deliberate attempt to murder," said Consul Lingford. "The law shall take its course. I don't know how precisely to deal with this Captain Dettmar, but if he comes to Attu-Attu, depend upon it he shall be dealt with, he—ah—shall be dealt with. In the meantime, I shall read up the law. And now, won't you and your good lady stop for lunch!"

As Duncan accepted the invitation, Minnie, who had been glancing out of the window at the harbor, suddenly leaned forward and touched her husband's arm. He followed her gaze, and saw the Samoset, flag at half mast, rounding up and dropping anchor scarcely a hundred yards away.

"There's my boat now," Duncan said to the Consul. "And there's the launch over the side, and Captain Dettmar dropping into it. If I don't miss my guess, he's coming to report our deaths to you."

The launch landed on the white beach, and leaving Lorenzo tinkering with the engine, Captain Dettmar strode across the beach and up the path to the Consulate.

"Let him make his report," Duncan said. "We'll just step into this next room and listen."

And through the partly open door, he and his wife heard Captain Dettmar, with tears in his voice, describe the loss of his owners.

"I jibed over and went back across the very spot," he concluded. "There was not a sign of them. I called and called, but there was never an answer. I tacked back and forth and wore for two solid hours, then hove to till daybreak, and cruised back and forth all day, two men at the mastheads. It is terrible. I am heartbroken. Mr. Duncan was a splendid man, and I shall never. . ."

But he never completed the sentence, for at that moment his splendid employer strode out upon him, leaving Minnie standing in the doorway. Captain Dettmar's white face blanched even whiter.

"I did my best to pick you up, sir," he began.

Boyd Duncan's answer was couched in terms of bunched knuckles, two bunches of them, that landed right and left on Captain Dettmar's face.

Captain Dettmar staggered backward, recovered, and rushed with swinging arms at his employer, only to be met with a blow squarely between the eyes. This time the Captain went down, bearing the typewriter under him as he crashed to the floor.

"This is not permissible," Consul Lingford spluttered. "I beg of you, I beg of you, to desist."

"I'll pay the damages to office furniture," Duncan answered, and at the same time landing more bunched knuckles on the eyes and nose of Dettmar.

Consul Lingford bobbed around in the turmoil like a wet hen, while his office furniture went to ruin. Once, he caught Duncan by the arm, but was flung back, gasping, half-across the room. Another time he appealed to Minnie.

"Mrs. Duncan, won't you, please, please, restrain your husband?"

But she, white-faced and trembling, resolutely shook her head and watched the fray with all her eyes.

"It is outrageous," Consul Lingford cried, dodging the hurtling bodies of the two men. "It is an affront to the Government, to the United States Government. Nor will it be overlooked, I warn you. Oh, do pray desist, Mr. Duncan. You will kill the man. I beg of you. I beg, I beg. . ."

But the crash of a tall vase filled with crimson hibiscus blossoms left him speechless.

The time came when Captain Dettmar could no longer get up. He got as far as hands and knees, struggled vainly to rise further, then collapsed. Duncan stirred the groaning wreck with his foot.

"He's all right," he announced. "I've only given him what he has given many a sailor and worse."

"Great heavens, sir!" Consul Lingford exploded, staring horror-stricken at the man whom he had invited to lunch.

Duncan giggled involuntarily, then controlled himself.

"I apologize, Mr. Lingford, I most heartily apologize. I fear I was slightly carried away by my feelings."

Consul Lingford gulped and sawed the air speechlessly with his arms.

"Slightly, sir? Slightly?" he managed to articulate.

"Boyd," Minnie called softly from the doorway.

He turned and looked.

"You *are* a joy," she said.

"And now, Mr. Lingford, I am done with him," Duncan said. "I turn over what is left to you and the law."

"That?" Consul Lingford queried, in accent of horror.

"That," Boyd Duncan replied, looking ruefully at his battered knuckles.

WAR

I

HE WAS A YOUNG MAN, not more than twenty-four or five, and he might have sat his horse with the careless grace of his youth had he not been so catlike and tense. His black eyes roved everywhere, catching the movements of twigs and branches where small birds hopped, questing ever onward through the changing vistas of trees and brush, and returning always to the clumps of undergrowth on either side. And as he watched, so did he listen, though he rode on in silence, save for the boom of heavy guns from far to the west. This had been sounding monotonously in his ears for hours, and only its cessation could have aroused his notice. For he had business closer to hand. Across his saddle-bow was balanced a carbine.

So tensely was he strung, that a bunch of quail, exploding into flight from under his horse's nose, startled him to such an extent that automatically, instantly, he had reined in and fetched the carbine halfway to his shoulder. He grinned sheepishly, recovered himself, and rode on. So tense was he, so bent upon the work he had to do, that the sweat stung his eyes unwiped, and unheeded rolled down his nose and spattered his saddle pommel. The band of his cavalryman's hat was fresh-stained with sweat. The roan horse under him was likewise wet. It was high noon of a breathless day of heat. Even the birds and squirrels did not dare the sun, but sheltered in shady hiding places among the trees.

Man and horse were littered with leaves and dusted with yellow pollen, for the open was ventured no more than was compulsory. They kept to the brush and trees, and invariably the man halted and peered out before crossing a dry glade or naked stretch of upland pasturage. He worked always to the north, though his way was devious, and it was from the north that he seemed most to apprehend that for which he was looking. He was no coward, but his courage was only that of the average civilized man, and he was looking to live, not die.

Up a small hillside he followed a cowpath through such dense scrub that he was forced to dismount and lead his horse. But when the path swung around to the west, he abandoned it and headed to the north again along the oak-covered top of the ridge.

The ridge ended in a steep descent-so steep that he zigzagged back and forth across the face of the slope, sliding and stumbling among the dead leaves and matted vines and keeping a watchful eye on the horse above that threatened to fall down upon him. The sweat ran from him, and the pollen-dust, settling pungently in mouth and nostrils, increased his thirst. Try as he would, nevertheless the descent was noisy, and frequently he stopped, panting in the dry heat and listening for any warning from beneath.

At the bottom he came out on a flat, so densely forested that he could not make out its extent. Here the character of the woods changed, and he was able to remount. Instead of the twisted hillside oaks, tall straight trees, big-trunked and prosperous, rose from the damp fat soil. Only here and there were thickets, easily avoided, while he encountered winding, park-like glades where the cattle had pastured in the days before war had run them off.

His progress was more rapid now, as he came down into the valley, and at the end of half an hour he halted at an ancient rail fence on the edge of a clearing. He did not like the openness of it, yet his path lay across to the fringe of trees that marked the banks of the stream. It was a mere quarter of a mile across that open, but the thought of venturing out in it was repugnant. A rifle, a score of them, a thousand, might lurk in that fringe by the stream.

Twice he essayed to start, and twice he paused. He was appalled by his own loneliness. The pulse of war that beat from the West suggested the companionship of battling thousands; here was naught but silence, and himself, and possible death-dealing bullets from a myriad ambushes. And yet his task was to find what he feared to find. He must on, and on, till somewhere, some time, he encountered another man, or other men, from the other side, scouting, as he was scouting, to make report, as he must make report, of having come in touch.

Changing his mind, he skirted inside the woods for a distance, and again peeped forth. This time, in the middle of the clearing, he saw a small farmhouse. There were no signs of life. No smoke curled from the chimney, not a barnyard fowl clucked and strutted. The kitchen door stood open, and he gazed so long and hard into the black aperture that it seemed almost that a farmer's wife must emerge at any moment.

He licked the pollen and dust from his dry lips, stiffened himself, mind and body, and rode out into the blazing sunshine. Nothing stirred. He went on past the house, and approached the wall of trees and bushes by the river's bank. One thought persisted maddeningly. It was of the crash into his body of a high-velocity bullet. It made him feel very fragile and defenseless, and he crouched lower in the saddle.

Tethering his horse in the edge of the wood, he continued a hundred yards on foot till he came to the stream. Twenty feet wide it was, without perceptible current, cool and inviting, and he was very thirsty. But he waited inside his screen of leafage, his eyes fixed on the screen on the opposite side. To make the wait endurable, he sat down, his carbine resting on his knees. The minutes passed, and slowly his tenseness relaxed. At last he decided there was no danger; but just as he prepared to part the bushes and bend down to the water, a movement among the opposite bushes caught his eye.

It might be a bird. But he waited. Again there was an agitation of the bushes, and then, so suddenly that it almost startled a cry from him, the bushes parted and a face peered out. It was a face covered with several weeks' growth of ginger-colored beard. The eyes were blue and wide apart, with laughter-wrinkles in the comers that showed despite the tired and anxious expression of the whole face.

All this he could see with microscopic clearness, for the distance was no more than twenty feet. And all this he saw in such brief time, that he saw it as he lifted his carbine to his shoulder. He glanced along the sights, and knew that he was gazing upon a man who was as good as dead. It was impossible to miss at such point blank range.

But he did not shoot. Slowly he lowered the carbine and watched. A hand, clutching a water-bottle, became visible and the ginger beard bent downward to fill the bottle. He could hear the gurgle of the water. Then arm and bottle and ginger beard disappeared behind the closing bushes. A long time he waited, when, with thirst unslaked, he crept back to his horse, rode slowly across the sun-washed clearing, and passed into the shelter of the woods beyond.

II

ANOTHER DAY, HOT AND BREATHLESS. A deserted farmhouse, large, with many outbuildings and an orchard, standing in a clearing. From the Woods, on a roan horse, carbine across pommel, rode the young man with the quick black eyes. He breathed with relief as he gained the house. That a fight had taken place here earlier in the season was evident. Clips and empty cartridges, tarnished with verdigris, lay on the ground, which, while wet, had been torn up by the hoofs of horses. Hard by the kitchen garden were graves, tagged and numbered. From the oak tree by the kitchen door, in tattered, weatherbeaten garments, hung the bodies of two men. The faces, shriveled and defaced, bore no likeness to the faces of men. The roan horse snorted beneath them, and the rider caressed and soothed it and tied it farther away.

Entering the house, he found the interior a wreck. He trod on empty cartridges as he walked from room to room to reconnoiter from the windows. Men had camped and slept everywhere, and on the floor of one room he came upon stains unmistakable where the wounded had been laid down.

Again outside, he led the horse around behind the barn and invaded the orchard. A dozen trees were burdened with ripe apples. He filled his pockets, eating while he picked. Then a thought came to him, and he glanced at the sun, calculating the time of his return to camp. He pulled off his shirt, tying the sleeves and making a bag. This he proceeded to fill with apples.

As he was about to mount his horse, the animal suddenly pricked up its ears. The man, too, listened, and heard, faintly, the thud of hoofs on soft earth. He crept to the corner of the barn and peered out. A dozen mounted men, strung out loosely, approaching from the opposite side of the clearing, were only a matter of a hundred yards or so away. They rode on to the house. Some dismounted, while others remained in the saddle as an earnest that their stay would be short. They seemed to be holding a council, for he could hear them talking excitedly in the detested tongue of the alien invader. The time passed, but they seemed unable to reach a decision. He put the carbine away in its boot, mounted, and waited impatiently, balancing the shirt of apples on the pommel.

He heard footsteps approaching, and drove his spurs so fiercely into the roan as to force a surprised groan from the animal as it leaped forward. At the corner of the barn he saw the intruder, a mere boy of nineteen or twenty for all of his uniform jump back to escape being run down. At the same moment the roan swerved and its rider caught a glimpse of the aroused men by the house. Some were springing from their horses, and he could see the rifles going to their shoulders. He passed the kitchen door and the dried corpses swinging in the shade, compelling his foes to run around the front of the house. A rifle cracked, and a second, but he was going fast, leaning forward, low in the saddle, one hand clutching the shirt of apples, the other guiding the horse.

The top bar of the fence was four feet high, but he knew his roan and leaped it at full career to the accompaniment of several scattered shots. Eight hundred yards straight away were the woods, and the roan was covering the distance with mighty strides. Every man was now firing. pumping their guns so rapidly that he no longer heard individual shots. A bullet went through his hat, but he was unaware, though he did know when another tore through the apples on the pommel. And he winced and ducked even lower when a third bullet, fired low, struck a stone between his horse's legs and ricochetted off through the air, buzzing and humming like some incredible insect.

The shots died down as the magazines were emptied, until, quickly, there was no more shooting. The young man was elated. Through that astonishing fusillade he had come unscathed. He glanced back. Yes, they had emptied their magazines. He could see several reloading. Others were running back behind the house for their horses. As he looked, two already mounted, came back into view around the corner, riding hard. And at the same moment, he saw the man with the unmistakable ginger beard kneel down on the ground, level his gun, and coolly take his time for the long shot.

The young man threw his spurs into the horse, crouched very low, and swerved in his flight in order to distract the other's aim. And still the shot did not come. With each jump of the horse, the woods sprang nearer. They were only two hundred yards away and still the shot was delayed.

And then he heard it, the last thing he was to hear, for he was dead ere he hit the ground in the long crashing fall from the saddle. And they, watching at the house, saw him fall, saw his body bounce when it struck the earth, and saw the burst of red-cheeked apples that rolled about him. They laughed at the unexpected eruption of apples, and clapped their hands in applause of the long shot by the man with the ginger beard.

Under the Deck Awnings

"Can any man—a gentleman, I mean—call a woman a pig?"

The little man flung this challenge forth to the whole group, then leaned back in his deck chair, sipping lemonade with an air commingled of certitude and watchful belligerence. Nobody made answer. They were used to the little man and his sudden passions and high elevations.

"I repeat, it was in my presence that he said a certain lady, whom none of you knows, was a pig. He did not say swine. He grossly said that she was a pig. And I hold that no man who is a man could possibly make such a remark about any woman."

Dr. Dawson puffed stolidly at his black pipe. Matthews, with knees hunched up and clasped by his arms, was absorbed in the flight of a gunie. Sweet, finishing his Scotch and soda, was questing about with his eyes for a deck steward.

"I ask you, Mr. Treloar, can any man call any woman a pig?"

Treloar, who happened to be sitting next to him, was startled by the abruptness of the attack, and wondered what grounds he had ever given the little man to believe that he could call a woman a pig.

"I should say," he began his hesitant answer, "that it—er—depends on the—er—the lady."

The little man was aghast.

"You mean. . . ?" he quavered.

"That I have seen female humans who were as bad as pigs—and worse."

There was a long pained silence. The little man seemed withered by the coarse brutality of the reply. In his face was unutterable hurt and woe.

"You have told of a man who made a not nice remark and you have classified him," Treloar said in cold, even tones. "I shall now tell you about a woman—I beg your pardon—a lady, and when I have finished I shall ask you to classify her. Miss Caruthers I shall call her, principally for the reason that it is not her name. It was on a P. & O. boat, and it occurred neither more nor less than several years ago.

"Miss Caruthers was charming. No; that is not the word. She was amazing. She was a young woman, and a lady. Her father was a certain high official whose name, if I mentioned it, would be immediately recognized by all of you. She was with her mother and two maids at the time, going out to join the old gentleman wherever you like to wish in the East.

"She, and pardon me for repeating, was amazing. It is the one adequate word. Even the most minor adjectives applicable to her are bound to be sheer superlatives. There was nothing she could not do better than any woman and than most men. Sing, play—bah!—as some rhetorician once said of old Nap, competition fled from her. Swim! She could have made a fortune and a name as a public performer. She was one of those rare women who can strip off all the frills of dress, and in simple swimming suit be more satisfying beautiful. Dress! She was an artist.

"But her swimming. Physically, she was the perfect woman—you know what I mean, not in the gross, muscular way of acrobats, but in all the delicacy of line and fragility of frame and texture. And combined with this, strength. How she could do it was the marvel. You know the wonder of a woman's arm—the fore arm, I mean; the sweet fading away from rounded biceps and hint of muscle, down through small elbow and firm soft swell to the wrist, small, unthinkably small and round and strong. This was hers. And yet, to see her swimming the sharp quick English overhand stroke, and getting somewhere with it, too, was—well, I understand anatomy and athletics and such things, and yet it was a mystery to me how she could do it.

"She could stay under water for two minutes. I have timed her. No man on board, except Dennitson, could capture as many coins as she with a single dive. On the forward main-deck was a big canvas tank with six feet of sea-water. We used to toss small coins into it. I have seen her dive from the bridge deck—no mean feat in itself—into that six-feet of water, and fetch up no less than forty-seven coins, scattered willy-nilly over the whole bottom of the tank. Dennitson, a quiet young Englishman, never exceeded her in this, though he made it a point always to tie her score.

"She was a sea-woman, true. But she was a land-woman, a horsewoman—a—she was the universal woman. To see her, all softness of soft dress, surrounded by half a dozen eager men, languidly careless of them all or flashing brightness and wit on them and at them and through them, one would fancy she was good for nothing else in the world. At such moments I have compelled myself to remember her score of forty-seven coins from the bottom of the swimming tank. But that was she, the everlasting, wonder of a woman who did all things well.

"She fascinated every betrousered human around her. She had me—and I don't mind confessing it—she bad me to heel along with the rest. Young puppies and old gray dogs who ought to have known better—oh, they all came up and crawled around her skirts and whined and fawned when she whistled. They were all guilty, from young Ardmore, a pink cherub of nineteen outward bound for some clerkship in the Consular Service, to old Captain Bentley, grizzled and sea-worn, and as emotional, to look at, as a Chinese joss. There was a nice middle-aged chap, Perkins, I believe, who forgot his wife was on board until Miss Caruthers sent him to the right about and back where he belonged.

"Men were wax in her hands. She melted them, or softly molded them, or incinerated them, as she pleased. There wasn't a steward, even, grand and remote as she was, who, at her bidding, would have hesitated to souse the Old Man himself with a plate of soup. You have all seen such women—a sort of world's desire to all men. As a man-conqueror she was supreme. She was a whip-lash, a sting and a flame, an electric spark. Oh, believe me, at times there were flashes of will that scorched through her beauty and seduction and smote a victim into blank and shivering idiocy and fear.

"And don't fail to mark, in the light of what is to come, that she was a prideful woman. Pride of race, pride of caste, pride of sex, pride of power—she had it all, a pride strange and wilful and terrible.

"She ran the ship, she ran the voyage, she ran everything, and she ran Dennitson. That he had outdistanced the pack even the least wise of us admitted. That she liked him, and that this feeling was growing, there was not a doubt. I am certain that she looked on him with kinder eyes than she had ever looked with on man before. We still worshiped, and were always hanging about waiting to be whistled up, though we knew that Dennitson was laps and laps ahead of us. What might have happened we shall never know, for we came to Colombo and something else happened.

"You know Colombo, and how the native boys dive for coins in the shark-infested bay. Of course, it is only among the ground sharks and fish sharks that they venture. It is almost uncanny the way they know sharks and can sense the presence of a real killer—a tiger shark, for instance, or a gray nurse strayed up from Australian waters. Let such a shark appear, and, long before the passengers can guess, every mother's son of them is out of the water in a wild scramble for safety.

"It was after tiffin, and Miss Caruthers was holding her usual court under the deck-awnings. Old Captain Bentley had just been whistled up, and had granted her what he never granted before. . . nor since—permission for the boys to come up on the promenade deck. You see, Miss Caruthers was a swimmer, and she was interested. She took up a collection of all our small change, and herself tossed it overside, singly and in handfuls, arranging the terms of the contests, chiding a miss, giving extra rewards to clever wins, in short, managing the whole exhibition.

"She was especially keen on their jumping. You know, jumping feet-first from a height, it is very difficult to hold the body perpendicularly while in the air. The center of gravity of the male body is high, and the tendency is to overtopple. But the little beggars employed a method which she declared was new to her and which she desired to learn. Leaping from the davits of the boat-deck above, they plunged downward, their faces and shoulders bowed forward, looking at the water. And only at the last moment did they abruptly straighten up and enter the water erect and true.

"It was a pretty sight. Their diving was not so good, though there was one of them who was excellent at it, as he was in all the other stunts. Some white man must have taught him, for he made the proper swan dive and did it as beautifully as I have ever seen it. You know, headfirst into the water, from a great height, the problem is to enter the water at the perfect angle. Miss the angle and it means at the least a twisted back and injury for life. Also, it has meant death for many a bungler. But this boy could do it—seventy feet I know he cleared in one dive from the rigging—clenched hands on chest, head thrown back, sailing more like a bird, upward and out, and out and down, body flat on the air so that if it struck the surface in that position it would be split in half like a herring. But the moment before the water is reached, the head drops forward, the hands go out and lock the arms in an arch in advance of the head, and the body curves gracefully downward and enters the water just right.

"This the boy did, again and again, to the delight of all of us, but particularly of Miss Caruthers. He could not have been a moment over twelve or thirteen, yet he was by far the cleverest of the gang. He was the favorite of his crowd, and its leader. Though there were a number older than he, they acknowledged his chieftaincy. He was a beautiful boy, a lithe young god in breathing bronze, eyes wide apart, intelligent and daring, a bubble, a mote, a beautiful flash and sparkle of life. You have seen wonderful glorious creatures—animals, anything, a leopard, a horse-restless, eager, too much alive ever to be still, silken of muscle, each slightest movement a benediction of grace, every action wild, untrammeled, and over all spilling out that intense vitality, that sheen and luster of living light. The boy had it. Life poured out of him almost in an effulgence. His skin glowed with it. It burned in his eyes. I swear I could almost hear it crackle from him. Looking at him, it was as if a whiff of ozone came to one's nostrils—so fresh and young was he, so resplendent with health, so wildly wild.

"This was the boy. And it was he who gave the alarm in the midst of the sport. The boys made a dash of it for the gangway platform, swimming the fastest strokes they knew, pellmell, floundering and splashing, fright in their faces, clambering out with jumps and surges, any way to get out, lending one another a hand to safety, till all were strung along the gangway and peering down into the water.

"'What is the matter?' asked Miss Caruthers.

"'A shark, I fancy,' Captain Bentley answered. 'Lucky little beggars that he didn't get one of them.'

"'Are they afraid of sharks?' she asked.

"'Aren't you?' he asked back."

She shuddered, looked overside at the water, and made a move.

"'Not for the world would I venture where a shark might be,' she said, and shuddered again. 'They are horrible! Horrible!'

"The boys came up on the promenade deck, clustering close to the rail and worshiping Miss Caruthers who had flung them such a wealth of backsheesh. The performance being over, Captain Bentley motioned to them to clear out. But she stopped him.

"'One moment, please, Captain. I have always understood that the natives are not afraid of sharks.'

"She beckoned the boy of the swan dive nearer to her, and signed to him to dive over again. He shook his head, and along with all his crew behind him laughed as if it were a good joke.

"'Shark,' he volunteered, pointing to the water.

"'No,' she said. 'There is no shark.'

"But he nodded his head positively, and the boys behind him nodded with equal positiveness.

"'No, no, no,' she cried. And then to us, 'Who'll lend me a half-crown and a sovereign!'

"Immediately the half dozen of us were presenting her with crowns and sovereigns, and she accepted the two coins from young Ardmore.

"She held up the half-crown for the boys to see. But there was no eager rush to the rail preparatory to leaping. They stood there grinning sheepishly. She offered the coin to each one individually, and each, as his turn came, rubbed his foot against his calf, shook his head, and grinned. Then she tossed the half-crown overboard. With wistful, regretful faces they watched its silver flight through the air, but not one moved to follow it.

"'Don't do it with the sovereign,' Dennitson said to her in a low voice.

"She took no notice, but held up the gold coin before the eyes of the boy of the swan dive.

"'Don't,' said Captain Bentley. 'I wouldn't throw a sick cat overside with a shark around.'

"But she laughed, bent on her purpose, and continued to dazzle the boy.

"'Don't tempt him,' Dennitson urged. 'It is a fortune to him, and he might go over after it.'

"'Wouldn't *you*?' she flared at him. 'If I threw it?'"

This last more softly.

Dennitson shook his head.

"'Your price is high,' she said. 'For how many sovereigns would you go?'

"'There are not enough coined to get me overside,' was his answer.

"She debated a moment, the boy forgotten in her tilt with Dennitson.

"'For me?' she said very softly.

"'To save your life—yes. But not otherwise.'

"She turned back to the boy. Again she held the coin before his eyes, dazzling him with the vastness of its value. Then she made as to toss it out, and, involuntarily, he made a half-movement toward the rail, but was checked by sharp cries of reproof from his companions. There was anger in their voices as well.

"'I know it is only fooling,' Dennitson said. 'Carry it as far as you like, but for heaven's sake don't throw it.'

"Whether it was that strange wilfulness of hers, or whether she doubted the boy could be persuaded, there is no telling. It was unexpected to all of us. Out from the shade of the awning the coin flashed golden in the blaze of sunshine and fell toward the sea in a glittering arch. Before a hand could stay him, the boy was over the rail and curving beautifully downward after the coin. Both were in the air at the same time. It was a pretty sight. The sovereign cut the water sharply, and at the very spot, almost at the same instant, with scarcely a splash, the boy entered.

"From the quicker-eyed black boys watching, came an exclamation. We were all at the railing. Don't tell me it is necessary for a shark to turn on its back. That one did not. In the clear water, from the height we were above it, we saw everything. The shark was a big brute, and with one drive he cut the boy squarely in half.

"There was a murmur or something from among us—who made it I did not know; it might have been I. And then there was silence. Miss Caruthers was the first to speak. Her face was deathly white.

"'I never dreamed,' she said, and laughed a short, hysterical laugh.

"All her pride was at work to give her control. She turned weakly toward Dennitson, and then, on from one to another of us. In her eyes was a terrible sickness, and her lips were trembling. We were brutes—oh, I know it, now that I look back upon it. But we did nothing.

"'Mr. Dennitson,' she said, 'Tom, won't you take me below!'

"He never changed the direction of his gaze, which was the bleakest I have ever seen in a man's face, nor did he move an eyelid. He took a cigarette from his case and lighted it. Captain Bentley made a nasty sound in his throat and spat overboard. That was all; that and the silence.

"She turned away and started to walk firmly down the deck. Twenty feet away, she swayed and thrust a hand against the wall to save herself. And so she went on, supporting herself against the cabins and walking very slowly." Treloar ceased. He turned his head and favored the little man with a look of cold inquiry.

"Well," he said finally. "Classify her."

The little man gulped and swallowed.

"I have nothing to say," he said. "I have nothing whatever to say."

To Kill a Man

Though dim night-lights burned, she moved familiarly through the big rooms and wide halls, seeking vainly the half-finished book of verse she had mislaid and only now remembered. When she turned on the lights in the drawing-room, she disclosed herself clad in a sweeping negligee gown of soft rose-colored stuff, throat and shoulders smothered in lace. Her rings were still on her fingers, her massed yellow hair had not yet been taken down. She was delicately, gracefully beautiful, with slender, oval face, red lips, a faint color in the cheeks, and blue eyes of the chameleon sort that at will stare wide with the innocence of childhood, go hard and gray and brilliantly cold, or flame up in hot wilfulness and mastery.

She turned the lights off and passed out and down the hall toward the morning room. At the entrance she paused and listened. From farther on had come, not a noise, but an impression of movement. She could have sworn she had not heard anything, yet something had been different. The atmosphere of night quietude had been disturbed. She wondered what servant could be prowling about. Not the butler, who was notorious for retiring early save on special occasion. Nor could it be her maid, whom she had permitted to go that evening.

Passing on to the dining-room, she found the door closed. Why she opened it and went on in, she did not know, except for the feeling that the disturbing factor, whatever it might be, was there. The room was in darkness, and she felt her way to the button and pressed. As the blaze of light flashed on, she stepped back and cried out. It was a mere "Oh!" and it was not loud.

FACING HER, ALONGSIDE THE BUTTON, flat against the wall, was a man. In his hand, pointed toward her, was a revolver. She noticed, even in the shock of seeing him, that the weapon was black and exceedingly long-barreled. She knew black and exceedingly long it for what it was, a Colt's. He was a medium-sized man, roughly clad, brown-eyed, and swarthy with sunburn. He seemed very cool. There was no wabble to the revolver and it was directed toward her stomach, not from an outstretched arm, but from the hip, against which the forearm rested.

"Oh," she said. "I beg your pardon. You startled me. What do you want?"

"I reckon I want to get out," he answered, with a humorous twitch to the lips. "I've kind of lost my way in this here shebang, and if you'll kindly show me the door I'll cause no trouble and sure vamoose."

"But what are you doing here?" she demanded, her voice touched with the sharpness of one used to authority.

"Plain robbing, Miss, that's all. I came snooping around to see what I could gather up. I thought you wan't to home, seein' as I saw you pull out with your old man in an auto. I reckon that must a ben your pa, and you're Miss Setliffe."

Mrs. Setliffe saw his mistake, appreciated the naive compliment, and decided not to undeceive him.

"How do you know I am Miss Setliffe?" she asked.

"This is old Setliffe's house, ain't it?"

She nodded.

"I didn't know he had a daughter, but I reckon you must be her. And now, if it ain't botherin' you too much, I'd sure be obliged if you'd show me the way out."

"But why should I? You are a robber, a burglar."

"If I wan't an ornery shorthorn at the business, I'd be accumulatin' them rings on your fingers instead of being polite," he retorted.

"I come to make a raise outa old Setliffe, and not to be robbing women-folks. If you get outa the way, I reckon I can find my own way out."

Mrs. Setliffe was a keen woman, and she felt that from such a man there was little to fear. That he was not a typical criminal, she was certain. From his speech she knew he was not of the cities, and she seemed to sense the wider, homelier air of large spaces.

"Suppose I screamed?" she queried curiously. "Suppose I made an outcry for help? You couldn't shoot me? . . . a woman?"

She noted the fleeting bafflement in his brown eyes. He answered slowly and thoughtfully, as if working out a difficult problem. "I reckon, then, I'd have to choke you and maul you some bad."

"A woman?"

"I'd sure have to," he answered, and she saw his mouth set grimly. "You're only a soft woman, but you see, Miss, I can't afford to go to jail. No, Miss, I sure can't. There's a friend of mine waitin' for me out West. He's in a hole, and I've got to help him out." The mouth shaped even more grimly. "I guess I could choke you without hurting you much to speak of."

Her eyes took on a baby stare of innocent incredulity as she watched him.

"I never met a burglar before," she assured him, "and I can't begin to tell you how interested I am."

"I'm not a burglar, Miss. Not a real one," he hastened to add as she looked her amused unbelief. "It looks like it, me being here in your house. But it's the first time I ever tackled such a job. I needed the money bad. Besides, I kind of look on it like collecting what's coming to me."

"I don't understand," she smiled encouragingly. "You came here to rob, and to rob is to take what is not yours."

"Yes, and no, in this here particular case. But I reckon I'd better be going now."

He started for the door of the dining-room, but she interposed, and a very beautiful obstacle she made of herself. His left hand went out as if to grip her, then hesitated. He was patently awed by her soft womanhood.

"There!" she cried triumphantly. "I knew you wouldn't."

The man was embarrassed.

"I ain't never manhandled a woman yet," he explained, "and it don't come easy. But I sure will, if you set to screaming."

"Won't you stay a few minutes and talk?" she urged. "I'm so interested. I should like to hear you explain how burglary is collecting what is coming to you."

He looked at her admiringly.

"I always thought women-folks were scairt of robbers," he confessed. "But you don't seem none."

She laughed gaily.

"There are robbers and robbers, you know. I am not afraid of you, because I am confident you are not the sort of creature that would harm a woman. Come, talk with me a while. Nobody will disturb us. I am all alone. My—father caught the night train to New York. The servants are all asleep. I should like to give you something to eat—women always prepare midnight suppers for the burglars they catch, at least they do in the magazine stories. But I don't know where to find the food. Perhaps you will have something to drink?"

He hesitated, and did not reply; but she could see the admiration for her growing in his eyes.

"You're not afraid?" she queried. "I won't poison you, I promise. I'll drink with you to show you it is all right."

"You sure are a surprise package of all right," he declared, for the first time lowering the weapon and letting it hang at his side. "No one don't need to tell me ever again that women-folks in cities is afraid. You ain't much—just a little soft pretty thing. But you've sure got the spunk. And you're trustful on top of it. There ain't many women, or men either, who'd treat a man with a gun the way you're treating me."

She smiled her pleasure in the compliment, and her face, was very earnest as she said:

"That is because I like your appearance. You are too decent-looking a man to be a robber. You oughtn't to do such things. If you are in bad luck you should go to work. Come, put away that nasty revolver and let us talk it over. The thing for you to do is to work."

"Not in this burg," he commented bitterly. "I've walked two inches off the bottom of my legs trying to find a job. Honest, I was a fine large man once. . . before I started looking for a job."

The merry laughter with which she greeted his sally obviously pleased him, and she was quick to note and take advantage of it. She moved directly away from the door and toward the sideboard.

"Come, you must tell me all about it while I get that drink for you. What will it be? Whisky?"

"Yes, ma'am," he said, as he followed her, though he still carried the big revolver at his side, and though he glanced reluctantly at the unguarded open door.

She filled a glass for him at the sideboard.

"I promised to drink with you," she said hesitatingly. "But I don't like whisky. I. . . I prefer sherry."

She lifted the sherry bottle tentatively for his consent.

"Sure," he answered, with a nod. "Whisky's a man's drink. I never like to see women at it. Wine's more their stuff."

She raised her glass to his, her eyes meltingly sympathetic.

"Here's to finding you a good position—"

But she broke off at sight of the expression of surprised disgust on his face. The glass, barely touched, was removed from his wry lips.

"What is the matter!" she asked anxiously. "Don't you like it? Have I made a mistake?"

"It's sure funny whisky. Tastes like it got burned and smoked in the making."

"Oh! How silly of me! I gave you Scotch. Of course you are accustomed to rye. Let me change it."

She was almost solicitiously maternal, as she replaced the glass with another and sought and found the proper bottle.

"Better?" she asked.

"Yes, ma'am. No smoke in it. It's sure the real good stuff. I ain't had a drink in a week. Kind of slick, that; oily, you know; not made in a chemical factory."

"You are a drinking man?" It was half a question, half a challenge.

"No, ma'am, not to speak of. I *have* rared up and ripsnorted at spells, but most unfrequent. But there is times when a good stiff jolt lands on the right spot kerchunk, and this is sure one of them. And now, thanking you for your kindness, ma'am, I'll just be a pulling along."

But Mrs. Setliffe did not want to lose her burglar. She was too poised a woman to possess much romance, but there was a thrill about the present situation that delighted her. Besides, she knew there was no danger. The man, despite his jaw and the steady brown eyes, was eminently tractable. Also, farther back in her consciousness glimmered the thought of an audience of admiring friends. It was too bad not to have that audience.

"You haven't explained how burglary, in your case, is merely collecting what is your own," she said. "Come, sit down, and tell me about it here at the table."

She maneuvered for her own seat, and placed him across the corner from her. His alertness had not deserted him, as she noted, and his eyes roved sharply about, returning always with smoldering admiration to hers, but never resting long. And she noted likewise that while she spoke he was intent on listening for other sounds than those of her voice. Nor had he relinquished the revolver, which lay at the corner of the table between them, the butt close to his right hand.

But he was in a new habitat which he did not know. This man from the West, cunning in woodcraft and plainscraft, with eyes and ears open, tense and suspicious, did not know that under the table, close to her foot, was the push button of an electric bell. He had never heard of such a contrivance, and his keenness and wariness went for naught.

"It's like this, Miss," he began, in response to her urging. "Old Setliffe done me up in a little deal once. It was raw, but it worked. Anything will work full and legal when it's got few hundred million behind it.

I'm not squealin', and I ain't taking a slam at your pa. He don't know me from Adam, and I reckon he don't know he done me outa anything. He's too big, thinking and dealing in millions, to ever hear of a small potato like me. He's an operator. He's got all kinds of experts thinking and planning and working for him, some of them, I hear, getting more cash salary than the President of the United States. I'm only one of thousands that have been done up by your pa, that's all.

"You see, ma'am, I had a little hole in the ground—a dinky, hydraulic, one-horse outfit of a mine. And when the Setliffe crowd shook down Idaho, and reorganized the smelter trust, and roped in the rest of the landscape, and put through the big hydraulic scheme at Twin Pines, why I sure got squeezed. I never had a run for my money. I was scratched off the card before the first heat. And so, to-night, being broke and my friend needing me bad, I just dropped around to make a raise outa your pa. Seeing as I needed it, it kinda was coming to me."

"Granting all that you say is so," she said, "nevertheless it does not make house-breaking any the less house-breaking. You couldn't make such a defense in a court of law."

"I know that," he confessed meekly. "What's right ain't always legal. And that's why I am so uncomfortable a-settin' here and talking with you. Not that I ain't enjoying your company—I sure do enjoy it—but I just can't afford to be caught. I know what they'd do to me in this here city. There was a young fellow that got fifty years only last week for holding a man up on the street for two dollars and eighty-five cents. I read about it in the paper. When times is hard and they ain't no work, men get desperate. And then the other men who've got something to be robbed of get desperate, too, and they just sure soak it to the other fellows. If I got caught, I reckon I wouldn't get a mite less than ten years. That's why I'm hankering to be on my way."

"No; wait." She lifted a detaining hand, at the same time removing her foot from the bell, which she had been pressing intermittently. "You haven't told me your name yet."

He hesitated.

"Call me Dave."

"Then. . . Dave," she laughed with pretty confusion. "Something must be done for you. You are a young man, and you are just at the beginning of a bad start. If you begin by attempting to collect what you think is coming to you, later on you will be collecting what you are perfectly sure isn't coming to you. And you know what the end will be. Instead of this, we must find something honorable for you to do."

"I need the money, and I need it now," he replied doggedly. "It's not for myself, but for that friend I told you about. He's in a peck of trouble, and he's got to get his lift now or not at all."

"I can find you a position," she said quickly. "And—yes, the very thing!—I'll lend you the money you want to send to your friend. This you can pay back out of your salary."

"About three hundred would do," he said slowly. "Three hundred would pull him through. I'd work my fingers off for a year for that, and my keep, and a few cents to buy Bull Durham with."

"Ah! You smoke! I never thought of it."

Her hand went out over the revolver toward his hand, as she pointed to the tell-tale yellow stain on his fingers. At the same time her eyes measured the nearness of her own hand and of his to the weapon. She ached to grip it in one swift movement. She was sure she could do it, and yet she was not sure; and so it was that she refrained as she withdrew her hand.

"Won't you smoke?" she invited.

"I'm 'most dying to."

"Then do so. I don't mind. I really like it—cigarettes, I mean."

With his left band he dipped into his side pocket, brought out a loose wheat-straw paper and shifted it to his right hand close by the revolver. Again he dipped, transferring to the paper a pinch of brown, flaky tobacco. Then he proceeded, both hands just over the revolver, to roll the cigarette.

"From the way you hover close to that nasty weapon, you seem to be afraid of me," she challenged.

"Not exactly afraid of you, ma'am, but, under the circumstances, just a mite timid."

"But I've not been afraid of you."

"You've got nothing to lose."

"My life," she retorted.

"That's right," he acknowledged promptly, "and you ain't been scairt of me. Mebbe I am over anxious."

"I wouldn't cause you any harm."

Even as she spoke, her slipper felt for the bell and pressed it. At the same time her eyes were earnest with a plea of honesty.

"You are a judge of men. I know it. And of women. Surely, when I am trying to persuade you from a criminal life and to get you honest work to do. . . ?"

He was immediately contrite.

"I sure beg your pardon, ma'am," he said. "I reckon my nervousness ain't complimentary."

As he spoke, he drew his right hand from the table, and after lighting the cigarette, dropped it by his side.

"Thank you for your confidence," she breathed softly, resolutely keeping her eyes from measuring the distance to the revolver, and keeping her foot pressed firmly on the bell.

"About that three hundred," he began. "I can telegraph it West tonight. And I'll agree to work a year for it and my keep."

"You will earn more than that. I can promise seventy-five dollars a month at the least. Do you know horses?"

His face lighted up and his eyes sparkled.

"Then go to work for me—or for my father, rather, though I engage all the servants. I need a second coachman—"

"And wear a uniform?" he interrupted sharply, the sneer of the freeborn West in his voice and on his lips.

She smiled tolerantly.

"Evidently that won't do. Let me think. Yes. Can you break and handle colts?"

He nodded.

"We have a stock farm, and there's room for just such a man as you. Will you take it?"

"Will I, ma'am?" His voice was rich with gratitude and enthusiasm. "Show me to it. I'll dig right in to-morrow. And I can sure promise you one thing, ma'am. You'll never be sorry for lending Hughie Luke a hand in his trouble—"

"I thought you said to call you Dave," she chided forgivingly.

"I did, ma'am. I did. And I sure beg your pardon. It was just plain bluff. My real name is Hughie Luke. And if you'll give me the address of that stock farm of yours, and the railroad fare, I head for it first thing in the morning."

Throughout the conversation she had never relaxed her attempts on the bell. She had pressed it in every alarming way—three shorts and a long, two and a long, and five. She had tried long series of shorts, and, once, she had held the button down for a solid three minutes. And she had been divided between objurgation of the stupid, heavy-sleeping butler and doubt if the bell were in order.

"I am so glad," she said; "so glad that you are willing. There won't be much to arrange. But you will first have to trust me while I go upstairs for my purse."

She saw the doubt flicker momentarily in his eyes, and added hastily, "But you see I am trusting you with the three hundred dollars."

"I believe you, ma'am," he came back gallantly. "Though I just can't help this nervousness."

"Shall I go and get it?"

But before she could receive consent, a slight muffled jar from the distance came to her ear. She knew it for the swing-door of the butler's pantry. But so slight was it—more a faint vibration than a sound—that she would not have heard had not her ears been keyed and listening for it. Yet the man had heard. He was startled in his composed way.

"What was that?" he demanded.

For answer, her left hand flashed out to the revolver and brought it back. She had had the start of him, and she needed it, for the next instant his hand leaped up from his side, clutching emptiness where the revolver had been.

"Sit down!" she commanded sharply, in a voice new to him. "Don't move. Keep your hands on the table."

She had taken a lesson from him. Instead of holding the heavy weapon extended, the butt of it and her forearm rested on the table, the muzzle pointed, not at his head, but his chest. And he, looking coolly and obeying her commands, knew there was no chance of the kick-up of the recoil producing a miss. Also, he saw that the revolver did not wabble, nor the hand shake, and he was thoroughly conversant with the size of hole the soft-nosed bullets could make. He had eyes, not for her, but for the hammer, which had risen under the pressure of her forefinger on the trigger.

"I reckon I'd best warn you that that there trigger-pull is filed dreadful fine. Don't press too hard, or I'll have a hole in me the size of a walnut."

She slacked the hammer partly down.

"That's better," he commented. "You'd best put it down all the way. You see how easy it works. If you want to, a quick light pull will jiffy her up and back and make a pretty mess all over your nice floor."

A door opened behind him, and he heard somebody enter the room. But he did not turn his head. He was looking at her, and he found it the face of another woman—hard, cold, pitiless yet brilliant in its beauty. The eyes, too, were hard, though blazing with a cold light.

"Thomas," she commanded, "go to the telephone and call the police. Why were you so long in answering?"

"I came as soon as I heard the bell, madam," was the answer.

The robber never took his eyes from hers, nor did she from his, but at mention of the bell she noticed that his eyes were puzzled for the moment.

"Beg your pardon," said the butler from behind, "but wouldn't it be better for me to get a weapon and arouse the servants?"

"No; ring for the police. I can hold this man. Go and do it—quickly."

The butler slippered out of the room, and the man and the woman sat on, gazing into each other's eyes. To her it was an experience keen with enjoyment, and in her mind was the gossip of her crowd, and she saw notes in the society weeklies of the beautiful young Mrs. Setliffe capturing an armed robber single-handed. It would create a sensation, she was sure.

"When you get that sentence you mentioned," she said coldly, "you will have time to meditate upon what a fool you have been, taking other persons' property and threatening women with revolvers. You will have time to learn your lesson thoroughly. Now tell the truth. You haven't any friend in trouble. All that you told me was lies."

He did not reply. Though his eyes were upon her, they seemed blank. In truth, for the instant she was veiled to him, and what he saw was the wide sunwashed spaces of the West, where men and women were bigger than the rotten denizens, as he had encountered them, of the thrice rotten cities of the East.

"Go on. Why don't you speak? Why don't you lie some more? Why don't you beg to be let off?"

"I might," he answered, licking his dry lips. "I might ask to be let off if. . ."

"If what?" she demanded peremptorily, as he paused.

"I was trying to think of a word you reminded me of. As I was saying, I might if you was a decent woman."

Her face paled.

"Be careful," she warned.

"You don't dast kill me," he sneered. "The world's a pretty low down place to have a thing like you prowling around in it, but it ain't so plumb low down, I reckon, as to let you put a hole in me. You're sure bad, but the trouble with you is that you're weak in your badness. It ain't much to kill a man, but you ain't got it in you. There's where you lose out."

"Be careful of what you say," she repeated. "Or else, I warn you, it will go hard with you. It can be seen to whether your sentence is light or heavy."

"Something's the matter with God," he remarked irrelevantly, "to be letting you around loose. It's clean beyond me what he's up to, playing such-like tricks on poor humanity. Now if I was God—"

His further opinion was interrupted by the entrance of the butler.

"Something is wrong with the telephone, madam," he announced. "The wires are crossed or something, because I can't get Central."

"Go and call one of the servants," she ordered. "Send him out for an officer, and then return here."

Again the pair was left alone.

"Will you kindly answer one question, ma'am?" the man said. "That servant fellow said something about a bell. I watched you like a cat, and you sure rung no bell."

"It was under the table, you poor fool. I pressed it with my foot."

"Thank you, ma'am. I reckoned I'd seen your kind before, and now I sure know I have. I spoke to you true and trusting, and all the time you was lying like hell to me."

She laughed mockingly.

"Go on. Say what you wish. It is very interesting."

"You made eyes at me, looking soft and kind, playing up all the time the fact that you wore skirts instead of pants—and all the time with your foot on the bell under the table. Well, there's some consolation. I'd sooner be poor Hughie Luke, doing his ten years, than be in your skin. Ma'am, hell is full of women like you."

There was silence for a space, in which the man, never taking his eyes from her, studying her, was making up his mind.

"Go on," she urged. "Say something."

"Yes, ma'am, I'll say something. I'll sure say something. Do you know what I'm going to do? I'm going to get right up from this chair and walk out that door. I'd take the gun from you, only you might turn foolish and let it go off. You can have the gun. It's a good one. As I was saying, I am going right out that door. And you ain't going to pull that gun off either. It takes guts to shoot a man, and you sure ain't got them. Now get ready and see if you can pull that trigger. I ain't going to harm you. I'm going out that door, and I'm starting."

Keeping his eyes fixed on her, he pushed back the chair and slowly stood erect. The hammer rose halfway. She watched it. So did he.

"Pull harder," he advised. "It ain't half up yet. Go on and pull it and kill a man. That's what I said, kill a man, spatter his brains out on the floor, or slap a hole into him the size of your fist. That's what killing a man means."

The hammer lowered jerkily but gently. The man turned his back and walked slowly to the door. She swung the revolver around so that it bore on his back. Twice again the hammer came up halfway and was reluctantly eased down.

At the door the man turned for a moment before passing on. A sneer was on his lips. He spoke to her in a low voice, almost drawling, but in it was the quintessence of all loathing, as he called her a name unspeakable and vile.

The Mexican

I

NOBODY KNEW HIS HISTORY—THEY OF the Junta least of all. He was their "little mystery," their "big patriot," and in his way he worked as hard for the coming Mexican Revolution as did they. They were tardy in recognizing this, for not one of the Junta liked him. The day he first drifted into their crowded, busy rooms, they all suspected him of being a spy—one of the bought tools of the Diaz secret service. Too many of the comrades were in civil an military prisons scattered over the United States, and others of them, in irons, were even then being taken across the border to be lined up against adobe walls and shot.

At the first sight the boy did not impress them favorably. Boy he was, not more than eighteen and not over large for his years. He announced that he was Felipe Rivera, and that it was his wish to work for the Revolution. That was all—not a wasted word, no further explanation. He stood waiting. There was no smile on his lips, no geniality in his eyes. Big dashing Paulino Vera felt an inward shudder. Here was something forbidding, terrible, inscrutable. There was something venomous and snakelike in the boy's black eyes. They burned like cold fire, as with a vast, concentrated bitterness. He flashed them from the faces of the conspirators to the typewriter which little Mrs. Sethby was industriously operating. His eyes rested on hers but an instant—she had chanced to look up—and she, too, sensed the nameless something that made her pause. She was compelled to read back in order to regain the swing of the letter she was writing.

Paulino Vera looked questioningly at Arrellano and Ramos, and questioningly they looked back and to each other. The indecision of doubt brooded in their eyes. This slender boy was the Unknown, vested with all the menace of the Unknown. He was unrecognizable, something quite beyond the ken of honest, ordinary revolutionists whose fiercest hatred for Diaz and his tyranny after all was only that of honest and ordinary patriots. Here was something else, they knew not what. But Vera, always the most impulsive, the quickest to act, stepped into the breach.

"Very well," he said coldly. "You say you want to work for the Revolution. Take off your coat. Hang it over there. I will show you, come—where are the buckets and cloths. The floor is dirty. You will begin by scrubbing it, and by scrubbing the floors of the other rooms. The spittoons need to be cleaned. Then there are the windows."

"Is it for the Revolution?" the boy asked.

"It is for the Revolution," Vera answered.

Rivera looked cold suspicion at all of them, then proceeded to take off his coat.

"It is well," he said.

And nothing more. Day after day he came to his work—sweeping, scrubbing, cleaning. He emptied the ashes from the stoves, brought up the coal and kindling, and lighted the fires before the most energetic one of them was at his desk.

"Can I sleep here?" he asked once.

Ah, ha! So that was it—the hand of Diaz showing through! To sleep in the rooms of the Junta meant access to their secrets, to the lists of names, to the addresses of comrades down on Mexican soil. The request was denied, and Rivera never spoke of it again. He slept they knew not where, and ate they knew not where nor how. Once, Arrellano offered him a couple of dollars. Rivera declined the money with a shake of the head. When Vera joined in and tried to press it upon him, he said:

"I am working for the Revolution."

It takes money to raise a modern revolution, and always the Junta was pressed. The members starved and toiled, and the longest day was none too long, and yet there were times when it appeared as if the Revolution stood or fell on no more than the matter of a few dollars. Once, the first time, when the rent of the house was two months behind and the landlord was threatening dispossession, it was Felipe Rivera, the scrub-boy in the poor, cheap clothes, worn and threadbare, who laid sixty dollars in gold on May Sethby's desk. There were other times. Three hundred letters, clicked out on the busy typewriters (appeals for assistance, for sanctions from the organized labor groups, requests for square news deals to the editors of newspapers, protests against the high-handed treatment of revolutionists by the United States courts), lay unmailed, awaiting postage. Vera's watch had disappeared—the old-fashioned gold repeater that had been his father's. Likewise had gone the plain gold band from May Setbby's third finger. Things were desperate. Ramos and Arrellano pulled their long mustaches in despair. The letters must go off, and the Post Office allowed no credit to purchasers of stamps. Then it was that Rivera put on his hat and went out. When he came back he laid a thousand two-cent stamps on May Sethby's desk.

"I wonder if it is the cursed gold of Diaz?" said Vera to the comrades.

They elevated their brows and could not decide. And Felipe Rivera, the scrubber for the Revolution, continued, as occasion arose, to lay down gold and silver for the Junta's use.

And still they could not bring themselves to like him. They did not know him. His ways were not theirs. He gave no confidences. He repelled all probing. Youth that he was, they could never nerve themselves to dare to question him.

"A great and lonely spirit, perhaps, I do not know, I do not know," Arrellano said helplessly.

"He is not human," said Ramos.

"His soul has been seared," said May Sethby. "Light and laughter have been burned out of him. He is like one dead, and yet he is fearfully alive."

"He has been through hell," said Vera. "No man could look like that who has not been through hell—and he is only a boy."

Yet they could not like him. He never talked, never inquired, never suggested. He would stand listening, expressionless, a thing dead, save for his eyes, coldly burning, while their talk of the Revolution ran high and warm. From face to face and speaker to speaker his eyes would turn, boring like gimlets of incandescent ice, disconcerting and perturbing.

"He is no spy," Vera confided to May Sethby. "He is a patriot—mark me, the greatest patriot of us all. I know it, I feel it, here in my heart and head I feel it. But him I know not at all."

"He has a bad temper," said May Sethby.

"I know," said Vera, with a shudder. "He has looked at me with those eyes of his. They do not love; they threaten; they are savage as a wild tiger's. I know, if I should prove unfaithful to the Cause, that he would kill me. He has no heart. He is pitiless as steel, keen and cold as frost. He is like moonshine in a winter night when a man freezes to death on some lonely mountain top. I am not afraid of Diaz and all his killers; but this boy, of him am I afraid. I tell you true. I am afraid. He is the breath of death."

Yet Vera it was who persuaded the others to give the first trust to Rivera. The line of communication between Los Angeles and Lower California had broken down. Three of the comrades had dug their own graves and been shot into them. Two more were United States prisoners in Los Angeles. Juan Alvarado, the Federal commander, was a monster. All their plans did he checkmate. They could no longer gain access to the active revolutionists, and the incipient ones, in Lower California.

Young Rivera was given his instructions and dispatched south. When he returned, the line of communication was reestablished, and Juan Alvarado was dead. He had been found in bed, a knife hilt-deep in his breast. This had exceeded Rivera's instructions, but they of the Junta knew the times of his movements. They did not ask him. He said nothing. But they looked at one another and conjectured.

"I have told you," said Vera. "Diaz has more to fear from this youth than from any man. He is implacable. He is the hand of God."

The bad temper, mentioned by May Sethby, and sensed by them all, was evidenced by physical proofs. Now he appeared with a cut lip, a blackened cheek, or a swollen ear. It was patent that he brawled, somewhere in that outside world where he ate and slept, gained money, and moved in ways unknown to them. As the time passed, he had come to set type for the little revolutionary sheet they published weekly. There were occasions when he was unable to set type, when his knuckles were bruised and battered, when his thumbs were injured and helpless, when one arm or the other hung wearily at his side while his face was drawn with unspoken pain.

"A wastrel," said Arrellano.

"A frequenter of low places," said Ramos.

"But where does he get the money?" Vera demanded. "Only to-day, just now, have I learned that he paid the bill for white paper—one hundred and forty dollars."

"There are his absences," said May Sethby. "He never explains them."

"We should set a spy upon him," Ramos propounded.

"I should not care to be that spy," said Vera. "I fear you would never see me again, save to bury me. He has a terrible passion. Not even God would he permit to stand between him and the way of his passion."

"I feel like a child before him," Ramos confessed.

"To me he is power—he is the primitive, the wild wolf, the striking rattlesnake, the stinging centipede," said Arrellano.

"He is the Revolution incarnate," said Vera. "He is the flame and the spirit of it, the insatiable cry for vengeance that makes no cry but that slays noiselessly. He is a destroying angel in moving through the still watches of the night."

"I could weep over him," said May Sethby. "He knows nobody. He hates all people. Us he tolerates, for we are the way of his desire. He is alone. . . lonely." Her voice broke in a half sob and there was dimness in her eyes.

Rivera's ways and times were truly mysterious. There were periods when they did not see him for a week at a time. Once, he was away a month. These occasions were always capped by his return, when, without advertisement or speech, he laid gold coins on May Sethby's desk. Again, for days and weeks, he spent all his time with the Junta. And yet again, for irregular periods, he would disappear through the heart of each day, from early morning until late afternoon. At such times he came early and remained late. Arrellano had found him at midnight, setting type with fresh swollen knuckles, or mayhap it was his lip, new-split, that still bled.

II

THE TIME OF THE CRISIS approached. Whether or not the Revolution would be depended upon the Junta, and the Junta was hard-pressed. The need for money was greater than ever before, while money was harder to get. Patriots had given their last cent and now could give no more. Section gang laborers-fugitive peons from Mexico—were contributing half their scanty wages. But more than that was needed. The heart-breaking, conspiring, undermining toil of years approached fruition. The time was ripe. The Revolution hung on the balance. One shove more, one last heroic effort, and it would tremble across the scales to victory. They knew their Mexico. Once started, the Revolution would take care of itself. The whole Diaz machine would go down like a house of cards. The border was ready to rise. One Yankee, with a hundred I.W.W. men, waited the word to cross over the border and begin the conquest of Lower California. But he needed guns. And clear across to the Atlantic, the Junta in touch with them all and all of them needing guns, mere adventurers, soldiers of fortune, bandits, disgruntled American union men, socialists, anarchists, rough-necks, Mexican exiles, peons escaped from bondage, whipped miners from the bull-pens of Coeur d'Alene and Colorado who desired only the more vindictively to fight—all the flotsam and jetsam of wild spirits from the madly complicated modern world. And it was guns and ammunition, ammunition and guns—the unceasing and eternal cry.

Fling this heterogeneous, bankrupt, vindictive mass across the border, and the Revolution was on. The custom house, the northern ports of entry, would be captured. Diaz could not resist. He dared not throw the weight of his armies against them, for he must hold the south. And through the south the flame would spread despite. The people would rise. The defenses of city after city would crumple up. State after state would totter down. And at last, from every side, the victorious armies of the Revolution would close in on the City of Mexico itself, Diaz's last stronghold.

But the money. They had the men, impatient and urgent, who would use the guns. They knew the traders who would sell and deliver the guns. But to culture the Revolution thus far had exhausted the Junta. The last dollar had been spent, the last resource and the last starving patriot milked dry, and the great adventure still trembled on the scales. Guns and ammunition! The ragged battalions must be armed. But how? Ramos lamented his confiscated estates. Arrellano wailed the spendthriftness of his youth. May Sethby wondered if it would have been different had they of the Junta been more economical in the past.

"To think that the freedom of Mexico should stand or fall on a few paltry thousands of dollars," said Paulino Vera.

Despair was in all their faces. Jose Amarillo, their last hope, a recent convert, who had promised money, had been apprehended at his hacienda in Chihuahua and shot against his own stable wall. The news had just come through.

Rivera, on his knees, scrubbing, looked up, with suspended brush, his bare arms flecked with soapy, dirty water.

"Will five thousand do it?" he asked.

They looked their amazement. Vera nodded and swallowed. He could not speak, but he was on the instant invested with a vast faith.

"Order the guns," Rivera said, and thereupon was guilty of the longest flow of words they had ever heard him utter. "The time is short. In three weeks I shall bring you the five thousand. It is well. The weather will be warmer for those who fight. Also, it is the best I can do."

Vera fought his faith. It was incredible. Too many fond hopes had been shattered since he had begun to play the revolution game. He believed this threadbare scrubber of the Revolution, and yet he dared not believe.

"You are crazy," he said.

"In three weeks," said Rivera. "Order the guns."

He got up, rolled down his sleeves, and put on his coat.

"Order the guns," he said.

"I am going now."

III

A<small>FTER HURRYING AND SCURRYING, MUCH</small> telephoning and bad language, a night session was held in Kelly's office. Kelly was rushed with business; also, he was unlucky. He had brought Danny Ward out from New York, arranged the fight for him with Billy Carthey, the date was three weeks away, and for two days now, carefully concealed from the sporting writers, Carthey had been lying up, badly injured. There was no one to take his place. Kelly had been burning the wires East to every eligible lightweight, but they were tied up with dates and contracts. And now hope had revived, though faintly.

"You've got a hell of a nerve," Kelly addressed Rivera, after one look, as soon as they got together.

Hate that was malignant was in Rivera's eyes, but his face remained impassive.

"I can lick Ward," was all he said.

"How do you know? Ever see him fight?"

Rivera shook his head.

"He can beat you up with one hand and both eyes closed."

Rivera shrugged his shoulders.

"Haven't you got anything to say?" the fight promoter snarled.

"I can lick him."

"Who'd you ever fight, anyway!" Michael Kelly demanded. Michael was the promotor's brother, and ran the Yellowstone pool rooms where he made goodly sums on the fight game.

Rivera favored him with a bitter, unanswering stare.

The promoter's secretary, a distinctively sporty young man, sneered audibly.

"Well, you know Roberts," Kelly broke the hostile silence. "He ought to be here. I've sent for him. Sit down and wait, though f rom the looks of you, you haven't got a chance. I can't throw the public down with a bum fight. Ringside seats are selling at fifteen dollars, you know that."

When Roberts arrived, it was patent that he was mildly drunk. He was a tall, lean, slack-jointed individual, and his walk, like his talk, was a smooth and languid drawl.

Kelly went straight to the point.

"Look here, Roberts, you've been bragging you discovered this little Mexican. You know Carthey's broke his arm. Well, this little yellow streak has the gall to blow in to-day and say he'll take Carthey's place. What about it?"

"It's all right, Kelly," came the slow response. "He can put up a fight."

"I suppose you'll be sayin' next that he can lick Ward," Kelly snapped.

Roberts considered judicially.

"No, I won't say that. Ward's a top-notcher and a ring general. But he can't hashhouse Rivera in short order. I know Rivera. Nobody can get his goat. He ain't got a goat that I could ever discover. And he's a two-handed fighter. He can throw in the sleep-makers from any position."

"Never mind that. What kind of a show can he put up? You've been conditioning and training fighters all your life. I take off my hat to your judgment. Can he give the public a run for its money?"

"He sure can, and he'll worry Ward a mighty heap on top of it. You don't know that boy. I do. I discovered him. He ain't got a goat. He's a devil. He's a wizzy-wooz if anybody should ask you. He'll make Ward sit up with a show of local talent that'll make the rest of you sit up. I won't say he'll lick Ward, but he'll put up such a show that you'll all know he's a comer."

"All right." Kelly turned to his secretary. "Ring up Ward. I warned him to show up if I thought it worth while. He's right across at the Yellowstone, throwin' chests and doing the popular."

Kelly turned back to the conditioner. "Have a drink?"

Roberts sipped his highball and unburdened himself.

"Never told you how I discovered the little cuss. It was a couple of years ago he showed up out at the quarters. I was getting Prayne ready for his fight with Delaney. Prayne's wicked. He ain't got a tickle of mercy in his make-up. I chopped up his pardner's something cruel, and I couldn't find a willing boy that'd work with him. I'd noticed this little starved Mexican kid hanging around, and I was desperate. So I grabbed him, shoved on the gloves and put him in. He was tougher'n rawhide, but weak. And he didn't know the first letter in the alphabet of boxing. Prayne chopped him to ribbons. But he hung on for two sickening rounds, when he fainted. Starvation, that was all. Battered! You couldn't have recognized him. I gave him half a dollar and a square meal. You oughta seen him wolf it down. He hadn't had the end of a bite for a couple of days. That's the end of him, thinks I. But next day he showed up, stiff an' sore, ready for another half and a square meal. And he done better as time went by. Just a born fighter, and tough beyond belief. He hasn't a heart. He's a piece of ice. And he never talked eleven words in a string since I know him. He saws wood and does his work."

"I've seen 'm," the secretary said. "He's worked a lot for you."

"All the big little fellows has tried out on him," Roberts answered. "And he's learned from 'em. I've seen some of them he could lick. But his heart wasn't in it. I reckoned he never liked the game. He seemed to act that way."

"He's been fighting some before the little clubs the last few months," Kelly said.

"Sure. But I don't know what struck 'm. All of a sudden his heart got into it. He just went out like a streak and cleaned up all the little local fellows. Seemed to want the money, and he's won a bit, though his clothes don't look it. He's peculiar. Nobody knows his business. Nobody knows how he spends his time. Even when he's on the job, he plumb up and disappears most of each day soon as his work is done. Sometimes he just blows away for weeks at a time. But he don't take advice. There's a fortune in it for the fellow that gets the job of managin' him, only he won't consider it. And you watch him hold out for the cash money when you get down to terms."

It was at this stage that Danny Ward arrived. Quite a party it was. His manager and trainer were with him, and he breezed in like a gusty draught of geniality, good-nature, and all-conqueringness. Greetings flew about, a joke here, a retort there, a smile or a laugh for everybody. Yet it was his way, and only partly sincere. He was a good actor, and he had found geniality a most valuable asset in the game of getting on in the world. But down underneath he was the deliberate, cold-blooded fighter and business man. The rest was a mask. Those who knew him or trafficked with him said that when it came to brass tacks he was Danny-on-the-Spot. He was invariably present at all business discussions, and it was urged by some that his manager was a blind whose only function was to serve as Danny's mouth-piece.

Rivera's way was different. Indian blood, as well as Spanish, was in his veins, and he sat back in a corner, silent, immobile, only his black eyes passing from face to face and noting everything.

"So that's the guy," Danny said, running an appraising eye over his proposed antagonist. "How de do, old chap."

Rivera's eyes burned venomously, but he made no sign of acknowledgment. He disliked all Gringos, but this Gringo he hated with an immediacy that was unusual even in him.

"Gawd!" Danny protested facetiously to the promoter. "You ain't expectin' me to fight a deef mute." When the laughter subsided, he made another hit. "Los Angeles must be on the dink when this is the best you can scare up. What kindergarten did you get 'm from?"

"He's a good little boy, Danny, take it from me," Roberts defended. "Not as easy as he looks."

"And half the house is sold already," Kelly pleaded. "You'll have to take 'm on, Danny. It is the best we can do."

Danny ran another careless and unflattering glance over Rivera and sighed.

"I gotta be easy with 'm, I guess. If only he don't blow up."

Roberts snorted.

"You gotta be careful," Danny's manager warned. "No taking chances with a dub that's likely to sneak a lucky one across."

"Oh, I'll be careful all right, all right," Danny smiled. "I'll get in at the start an' nurse 'im along for the dear public's sake. What d' ye say to fifteen rounds, Kelly—an' then the hay for him?"

"That'll do," was the answer. "As long as you make it realistic."

"Then let's get down to biz." Danny paused and calculated. "Of course, sixty-five per cent of the gate receipts, same as with Carthey. But the split'll be different. Eighty will just about suit me." And to his manager, "That right?"

The manager nodded.

"Here, you, did you get that?" Kelly asked Rivera.

Rivera shook his head.

"Well, it is this way," Kelly exposited. "The purse'll be sixty-five per cent of the gate receipts. You're a dub, and an unknown. You and Danny split, twenty per cent goin' to you, an' eighty to Danny. That's fair, isn't it, Roberts?"

"Very fair, Rivera," Roberts agreed.

"You see, you ain't got a reputation yet."

"What will sixty-five per cent of the gate receipts be?" Rivera demanded.

"Oh, maybe five thousand, maybe as high as eight thousand," Danny broke in to explain. "Something like that. Your share'll come to something like a thousand or sixteen hundred. Pretty good for takin' a licking from a guy with my reputation. What d' ye say?"

Then Rivera took their breaths away. "Winner takes all," he said with finality.

A dead silence prevailed.

"It's like candy from a baby," Danny's manager proclaimed.

Danny shook his head.

"I've been in the game too long," he explained.

"I'm not casting reflections on the referee, or the present company. I'm not sayin' nothing about book-makers an' frame-ups that sometimes happen. But what I do say is that it's poor business for a fighter like me. I play safe. There's no tellin'. Mebbe I break my arm, eh? Or some guy slips me a bunch of dope?" He shook his head solemnly. "Win or lose, eighty is my split. What d' ye say, Mexican?"

Rivera shook his head.

Danny exploded. He was getting down to brass tacks now.

"Why, you dirty little greaser! I've a mind to knock your block off right now."

Roberts drawled his body to interposition between hostilities.

"Winner takes all," Rivera repeated sullenly.

"Why do you stand out that way?" Danny asked.

"I can lick you," was the straight answer.

Danny half started to take off his coat. But, as his manager knew, it was a grand stand play. The coat did not come off, and Danny allowed himself to be placated by the group. Everybody sympathized with him. Rivera stood alone.

"Look here, you little fool," Kelly took up the argument. "You're nobody. We know what you've been doing the last few months—putting away little local fighters. But Danny is class. His next fight after this will be for the championship. And you're unknown. Nobody ever heard of you out of Los Angeles."

"They will," Rivera answered with a shrug, "after this fight."

"You think for a second you can lick me?" Danny blurted in.

Rivera nodded.

"Oh, come; listen to reason," Kelly pleaded. "Think of the advertising."

"I want the money," was Rivera's answer.

"You couldn't win from me in a thousand years," Danny assured him.

"Then what are you holdin' out for?" Rivera countered. "If the money's that easy, why don't you go after it?"

"I will, so help me!" Danny cried with abrupt conviction. "I'll beat you to death in the ring, my boy—you monkeyin' with me this way. Make out the articles, Kelly. Winner take all. Play it up in the sportin' columns. Tell 'em it's a grudge fight. I'll show this fresh kid a few."

Kelly's secretary had begun to write, when Danny interrupted.

"Hold on!" He turned to Rivera.

"Weights?"

"Ringside," came the answer.

"Not on your life, Fresh Kid. If winner takes all, we weigh in at ten A.M."

"And winner takes all?" Rivera queried.

Danny nodded. That settled it. He would enter the ring in his full ripeness of strength.

"Weigh in at ten," Rivera said.

The secretary's pen went on scratching.

"It means five pounds," Roberts complained to Rivera.

"You've given too much away. You've thrown the fight right there. Danny'll lick you sure. He'll be as strong as a bull. You're a fool. You ain't got the chance of a dewdrop in hell."

Rivera's answer was a calculated look of hatred. Even this Gringo he despised, and him had he found the whitest Gringo of them all.

IV

BARELY NOTICED WAS RIVERA AS he entered the ring. Only a very slight and very scattering ripple of half-hearted hand-clapping greeted him. The house did not believe in him. He was the lamb led to slaughter at the hands of the great Danny. Besides, the house was disappointed. It had expected a rushing battle between Danny Ward and Billy Carthey, and here it must put up with this poor little tyro. Still further, it had manifested its disapproval of the change by betting two, and even three, to one on Danny. And where a betting audience's money is, there is its heart.

The Mexican boy sat down in his corner and waited. The slow minutes lagged by. Danny was making him wait. It was an old trick, but ever it worked on the young, new fighters. They grew frightened, sitting thus and facing their own apprehensions and a callous, tobacco-smoking audience. But for once the trick failed. Roberts was right. Rivera had no goat. He, who was more delicately coordinated, more finely nerved and strung than any of them, had no nerves of this sort. The atmosphere of foredoomed defeat in his own corner had no effect on him. His handlers were Gringos and strangers. Also they were scrubs—the dirty driftage of the fight game, without honor, without efficiency. And they were chilled, as well, with certitude that theirs was the losing corner.

"Now you gotta be careful," Spider Hagerty warned him. Spider was his chief second. "Make it last as long as you can—them's my instructions from Kelly. If you don't, the papers'll call it another bum fight and give the game a bigger black eye in Los Angeles."

All of which was not encouraging. But Rivera took no notice. He despised prize fighting. It was the hated game of the hated Gringo. He had taken up with it, as a chopping block for others in the training quarters, solely because he was starving. The fact that he was marvelously made for it had meant nothing. He hated it. Not until he had come in to the Junta, had he fought for money, and he had found the money easy. Not first among the sons of men had he been to find himself successful at a despised vocation.

He did not analyze. He merely knew that he must win this fight. There could be no other outcome. For behind him, nerving him to this belief, were profounder forces than any the crowded house dreamed. Danny Ward fought for money, and for the easy ways of life that money would bring. But the things Rivera fought for burned in his brain— blazing and terrible visions, that, with eyes wide open, sitting lonely in the corner of the ring and waiting for his tricky antagonist, he saw as clearly as he had lived them.

He saw the white-walled, water-power factories of Rio Blanco. He saw the six thousand workers, starved and wan, and the little children, seven and eight years of age, who toiled long shifts for ten cents a day. He saw the perambulating corpses, the ghastly death's heads of men who labored in the dye-rooms. He remembered that he had heard his father call the dye-rooms the "suicide-holes," where a year was death. He saw the little patio, and his mother cooking and moiling at crude housekeeping and finding time to caress and love him. And his father he saw, large, big-moustached and deep-chested, kindly above all men, who loved all men and whose heart was so large that there was love to overflowing still left for the mother and the little muchacho playing in the corner of the patio. In those days his name had not been Felipe Rivera. It had been Fernandez, his father's and mother's name. Him had they called Juan. Later, he had changed it himself, for he had found the name of Fernandez hated by prefects of police, jefes politicos, and rurales.

Big, hearty Joaquin Fernandez! A large place he occupied in Rivera's visions. He had not understood at the time, but looking back he could understand. He could see him setting type in the little printery, or scribbling endless hasty, nervous lines on the much-cluttered desk. And he could see the strange evenings, when workmen, coming secretly in the dark like men who did ill deeds, met with his father and talked long hours where he, the muchacho, lay not always asleep in the corner.

As from a remote distance he could hear Spider Hagerty saying to him: "No layin' down at the start. Them's instructions. Take a beatin' and earn your dough."

Ten minutes had passed, and he still sat in his corner. There were no signs of Danny, who was evidently playing the trick to the limit.

But more visions burned before the eye of Rivera's memory. The strike, or, rather, the lockout, because the workers of Rio Blanco had helped their striking brothers of Puebla. The hunger, the expeditions in the hills for berries, the roots and herbs that all ate and that twisted and pained the stomachs of all of them. And then, the nightmare; the waste of ground before the company's store; the thousands of starving workers; General Rosalio Martinez and the soldiers of Porfirio Diaz, and the death-spitting rifles that seemed never to cease spitting, while the workers' wrongs were washed and washed again in their own blood. And that night! He saw the flat cars, piled high with the bodies of the slain, consigned to Vera Cruz, food for the sharks of the bay. Again he crawled over the grisly heaps, seeking and finding, stripped and mangled, his father and his mother. His mother he especially remembered—only her face projecting, her body burdened by the weight of dozens of bodies. Again the rifles of the soldiers of Porfirio Diaz cracked, and again he dropped to the ground and slunk away like some hunted coyote of the hills.

To his ears came a great roar, as of the sea, and he saw Danny Ward, leading his retinue of trainers and seconds, coming down the center aisle. The house was in wild uproar for the popular hero who was bound to win. Everybody proclaimed him. Everybody was for him. Even Rivera's own seconds warmed to something akin to cheerfulness when Danny ducked jauntily through the ropes and entered the ring. His face continually spread to an unending succession of smiles, and when Danny smiled he smiled in every feature, even to the laughter-wrinkles of the corners of the eyes and into the depths of the eyes themselves. Never was there so genial a fighter. His face was a running advertisement of good feeling, of good fellowship. He knew everybody. He joked, and laughed, and greeted his friends through the ropes. Those farther away, unable to suppress their admiration, cried loudly: "Oh, you Danny!" It was a joyous ovation of affection that lasted a full five minutes.

Rivera was disregarded. For all that the audience noticed, he did not exist. Spider Lagerty's bloated face bent down close to his.

"No gettin' scared," the Spider warned.

"An' remember instructions. You gotta last. No layin' down. If you lay down, we got instructions to beat you up in the dressing rooms. Savve? You just gotta fight."

The house began to applaud. Danny was crossing the ring to him. Danny bent over, caught Rivera's right hand in both his own and shook it with impulsive heartiness. Danny's smile-wreathed face was close to his. The audience yelled its appreciation of Danny's display of sporting spirit. He was greeting his opponent with the fondness of a brother. Danny's lips moved, and the audience, interpreting the unheard words to be those of a kindly-natured sport, yelled again. Only Rivera heard the low words.

"You little Mexican rat," hissed from between Danny's gaily smiling lips, "I'll fetch the yellow outa you."

Rivera made no move. He did not rise. He merely hated with his eyes.

"Get up, you dog!" some man yelled through the ropes from behind.

The crowd began to hiss and boo him for his unsportsmanlike conduct, but he sat unmoved. Another great outburst of applause was Danny's as he walked back across the ring.

When Danny stripped, there was ohs! and ahs! of delight. His body was perfect, alive with easy suppleness and health and strength. The skin was white as a woman's, and as smooth. All grace, and resilience, and power resided therein. He had proved it in scores of battles. His photographs were in all the physical culture magazines.

A groan went up as Spider Hagerty peeled Rivera's sweater over his head. His body seemed leaner, because of the swarthiness of the skin. He had muscles, but they made no display like his opponent's. What the audience neglected to see was the deep chest. Nor could it guess the toughness of the fiber of the flesh, the instantaneousness of the cell explosions of the muscles, the fineness of the nerves that wired every part of him into a splendid fighting mechanism. All the audience saw was a brown-skinned boy of eighteen with what seemed the body of a boy. With Danny it was different. Danny was a man of twenty-four, and his body was a man's body. The contrast was still more striking as they stood together in the center of the ring receiving the referee's last instructions.

Rivera noticed Roberts sitting directly behind the newspaper men. He was drunker than usual, and his speech was correspondingly slower.

"Take it easy, Rivera," Roberts drawled.

"He can't kill you, remember that. He'll rush you at the go-off, but don't get rattled. You just and stall, and clinch. He can't hurt cover up, much. Just make believe to yourself that he's choppin' out on you at the trainin' quarters."

Rivera made no sign that he had heard.

"Sullen little devil," Roberts muttered to the man next to him. "He always was that way."

But Rivera forgot to look his usual hatred. A vision of countless rifles blinded his eyes. Every face in the audience, far as he could see, to the high dollar-seats, was transformed into a rifle. And he saw the long Mexican border arid and sun-washed and aching, and along it he saw the ragged bands that delayed only for the guns.

Back in his corner he waited, standing up. His seconds had crawled out through the ropes, taking the canvas stool with them. Diagonally across the squared ring, Danny faced him. The gong struck, and the battle was on. The audience howled its delight. Never had it seen a battle open more convincingly. The papers were right. It was a grudge fight. Three-quarters of the distance Danny covered in the rush to get together, his intention to eat up the Mexican lad plainly advertised. He assailed with not one blow, nor two, nor a dozen. He was a gyroscope of blows, a whirlwind of destruction. Rivera was nowhere. He was overwhelmed, buried beneath avalanches of punches delivered from every angle and position by a past master in the art. He was overborne, swept back against the ropes, separated by the referee, and swept back against the ropes again.

It was not a fight. It was a slaughter, a massacre. Any audience, save a prize fighting one, would have exhausted its emotions in that first minute. Danny was certainly showing what he could do—a splendid exhibition. Such was the certainty of the audience, as well as its excitement and favoritism, that it failed to take notice that the Mexican still stayed on his feet. It forgot Rivera. It rarely saw him, so closely was he enveloped in Danny's man-eating attack. A minute of this went by, and two minutes. Then, in a separation, it caught a clear glimpse of the Mexican. His lip was cut, his nose was bleeding. As he turned and staggered into a clinch, the welts of oozing blood, from his contacts with the ropes, showed in red bars across his back. But what the audience did not notice was that his chest was not heaving and that his eyes were coldly burning as ever. Too many aspiring champions, in the cruel welter of the training camps, had practiced this man-eating attack on him. He had learned to live through for a compensation of from half a dollar a go up to fifteen dollars a week—a hard school, and he was schooled hard.

Then happened the amazing thing. The whirling, blurring mix-up ceased suddenly. Rivera stood alone. Danny, the redoubtable Danny, lay on his back. His body quivered as consciousness strove to return to it. He had not staggered and sunk down, nor had he gone over in a long slumping fall. The right hook of Rivera had dropped him in midair with the abruptness of death. The referee shoved Rivera back with one hand, and stood over the fallen gladiator counting the seconds. It is the custom of prize-fighting audiences to cheer a clean knock-down blow. But this audience did not cheer. The thing had been too unexpected. It watched the toll of the seconds in tense silence, and through this silence the voice of Roberts rose exultantly:

"I told you he was a two-handed fighter!"

By the fifth second, Danny was rolling over on his face, and when seven was counted, he rested on one knee, ready to rise after the count of nine and before the count of ten. If his knee still touched the floor at "ten," he was considered "down," and also "out." The instant his knee left the floor, he was considered "up," and in that instant it was Rivera's right to try and put him down again. Rivera took no chances. The moment that knee left the floor he would strike again. He circled around, but the referee circled in between, and Rivera knew that the seconds he counted were very slow. All Gringos were against him, even the referee.

At "nine" the referee gave Rivera a sharp thrust back. It was unfair, but it enabled Danny to rise, the smile back on his lips. Doubled partly over, with arms wrapped about face and abdomen, he cleverly stumbled into a clinch. By all the rules of the game the referee should have broken it, but he did not, and Danny clung on like a surf-battered barnacle and moment by moment recuperated. The last minute of the round was going fast. If he could live to the end, he would have a full minute in his corner to revive. And live to the end he did, smiling through all desperateness and extremity.

"The smile that won't come off!" somebody yelled, and the audience laughed loudly in its relief.

"The kick that Greaser's got is something God-awful," Danny gasped in his corner to his adviser while his handlers worked frantically over him.

The second and third rounds were tame. Danny, a tricky and consummate ring general, stalled and blocked and held on, devoting himself to recovering from that dazing first-round blow. In the fourth round he was himself again. Jarred and shaken, nevertheless his good condition had enabled him to regain his vigor. But he tried no man-eating tactics. The Mexican had proved a tartar. Instead, he brought to bear his best fighting powers. In tricks and skill and experience he was the master, and though he could land nothing vital, he proceeded scientifically to chop and wear down his opponent. He landed three blows to Rivera's one, but they were punishing blows only, and not deadly. It was the sum of many of them that constituted deadliness. He was respectful of this two-handed dub with the amazing short-arm kicks in both his fists.

In defense, Rivera developed a disconcerting straight-left. Again and again, attack after attack he straight-lefted away from him with accumulated damage to Danny's mouth and nose. But Danny was protean. That was why he was the coming champion. He could change from style to style of fighting at will. He now devoted himself to infighting. In this he was particularly wicked, and it enabled him to avoid the other's straight-left. Here he set the house wild repeatedly, capping it with a marvelous lockbreak and lift of an inside upper-cut that raised the Mexican in the air and dropped him to the mat. Rivera rested on one knee, making the most of the count, and in the soul of him he knew the referee was counting short seconds on him.

Again, in the seventh, Danny achieved the diabolical inside uppercut. He succeeded only in staggering Rivera, but, in the ensuing moment of defenseless helplessness, he smashed him with another blow through the ropes. Rivera's body bounced on the heads of the newspaper men below, and they boosted him back to the edge of the platform outside the ropes. Here he rested on one knee, while the referee raced off the seconds. Inside the ropes, through which he must duck to enter the ring, Danny waited for him. Nor did the referee intervene or thrust Danny back.

The house was beside itself with delight.

"Kill'm, Danny, kill'm!" was the cry.

Scores of voices took it up until it was like a war-chant of wolves.

Danny did his best, but Rivera, at the count of eight, instead of nine, came unexpectedly through the ropes and safely into a clinch. Now the referee worked, tearing him away so that he could be hit, giving Danny every advantage that an unfair referee can give.

But Rivera lived, and the daze cleared from his brain. It was all of a piece. They were the hated Gringos and they were all unfair. And in the worst of it visions continued to flash and sparkle in his brain— long lines of railroad track that simmered across the desert; rurales and American constables, prisons and calabooses; tramps at water tanks— all the squalid and painful panorama of his odyssey after Rio Blanca and the strike. And, resplendent and glorious, he saw the great, red Revolution sweeping across his land. The guns were there before him. Every hated face was a gun. It was for the guns he fought. He was the guns. He was the Revolution. He fought for all Mexico.

The audience began to grow incensed with Rivera. Why didn't he take the licking that was appointed him? Of course he was going to be licked, but why should he be so obstinate about it? Very few were interested in him, and they were the certain, definite percentage of a gambling crowd that plays long shots. Believing Danny to be the winner, nevertheless they had put their money on the Mexican at four to ten and one to three. More than a trifle was up on the point of how many rounds Rivera could last. Wild money had appeared at the ringside proclaiming that he could not last seven rounds, or even six. The winners of this, now that their cash risk was happily settled, had joined in cheering on the favorite.

Rivera refused to be licked. Through the eighth round his opponent strove vainly to repeat the uppercut. In the ninth, Rivera stunned the house again. In the midst of a clinch he broke the lock with a quick, lithe movement, and in the narrow space between their bodies his right lifted from the waist. Danny went to the floor and took the safety of the count. The crowd was appalled. He was being bested at his own game. His famous right-uppercut had been worked back on him. Rivera made no attempt to catch him as he arose at "nine." The referee was openly blocking that play, though he stood clear when the situation was reversed and it was Rivera who desired to rise.

Twice in the tenth, Rivera put through the right-uppercut, lifted from waist to opponent's chin. Danny grew desperate. The smile never left his face, but he went back to his man-eating rushes. Whirlwind as he would, he could not damage Rivera, while Rivera through the blur and whirl, dropped him to the mat three times in succession. Danny did not recuperate so quickly now, and by the eleventh round he was in a serious way. But from then till the fourteenth he put up the gamest exhibition of his career. He stalled and blocked, fought parsimoniously, and strove to gather strength. Also, he fought as foully as a successful fighter knows how. Every trick and device he employed, butting in the clinches with the seeming of accident, pinioning Rivera's glove between arm and body, heeling his glove on Rivera's mouth to clog his breathing. Often, in the clinches, through his cut and smiling lips he snarled insults unspeakable and vile in Rivera's ear. Everybody, from the referee to the house, was with Danny and was helping Danny. And they knew what he had in mind. Bested by this surprise-box of an unknown, he was pinning all on a single punch. He offered himself for punishment, fished, and feinted, and drew, for that one opening that would enable him to whip a blow through with all his strength and turn the tide. As another and greater fighter had done before him, he might do a right and left, to solar plexus and across the jaw. He could do it, for he was noted for the strength of punch that remained in his arms as long as he could keep his feet.

Rivera's seconds were not half-caring for him in the intervals between rounds. Their towels made a showing, but drove little air into his panting lungs. Spider Hagerty talked advice to him, but Rivera knew it was wrong advice. Everybody was against him. He was surrounded by treachery. In the fourteenth round he put Danny down again, and himself stood resting, hands dropped at side, while the referee counted. In the other corner Rivera had been noting suspicious whisperings. He saw Michael Kelly make his way to Roberts and bend and whisper. Rivera's ears were a cat's, desert-trained, and he caught snatches of what was said. He wanted to hear more, and when his opponent arose he maneuvered the fight into a clinch over against the ropes.

"Got to," he could hear Michael, while Roberts nodded. "Danny's got to win—I stand to lose a mint—I've got a ton of money covered—my own. If he lasts the fifteenth I'm bust—the boy'll mind you. Put something across."

And thereafter Rivera saw no more visions. They were trying to job him. Once again he dropped Danny and stood resting, his hands at his slide. Roberts stood up.

"That settled him," he said.

"Go to your corner."

He spoke with authority, as he had often spoken to Rivera at the training quarters. But Rivera looked hatred at him and waited for Danny to rise. Back in his corner in the minute interval, Kelly, the promoter, came and talked to Rivera.

"Throw it, damn you," he rasped in, a harsh low voice. "You gotta lay down, Rivera. Stick with me and I'll make your future. I'll let you lick Danny next time. But here's where you lay down."

Rivera showed with his eyes that he heard, but he made neither sign of assent nor dissent.

"Why don't you speak?" Kelly demanded angrily.

"You lose, anyway," Spider Hagerty supplemented. "The referee'll take it away from you. Listen to Kelly, and lay down."

"Lay down, kid," Kelly pleaded, "and I'll help you to the championship."

Rivera did not answer.

"I will, so help me, kid."

At the strike of the gong Rivera sensed something impending. The house did not. Whatever it was it was there inside the ring with him and very close. Danny's earlier surety seemed returned to him. The confidence of his advance frightened Rivera. Some trick was about to be worked. Danny rushed, but Rivera refused the encounter. He side-stepped away into safety. What the other wanted was a clinch. It was in some way necessary to the trick. Rivera backed and circled away, yet he knew, sooner or later, the clinch and the trick would come. Desperately he resolved to draw it. He made as if to effect the clinch with Danny's next rush. Instead, at the last instant, just as their bodies should have come together, Rivera darted nimbly back. And in the same instant Danny's corner raised a cry of foul. Rivera had fooled them. The referee paused irresolutely. The decision that trembled on his lips was never uttered, for a shrill, boy's voice from the gallery piped, "Raw work!"

Danny cursed Rivera openly, and forced him, while Rivera danced away. Also, Rivera made up his mind to strike no more blows at the body. In this he threw away half his chance of winning, but he knew if he was to win at all it was with the outfighting that remained to him. Given the least opportunity, they would lie a foul on him. Danny threw all caution to the winds. For two rounds he tore after and into the boy who dared not meet him at close quarters. Rivera was struck again and again; he took blows by the dozens to avoid the perilous clinch. During this supreme final rally of Danny's the audience rose to its feet and went mad. It did not understand. All it could see was that its favorite was winning, after all.

"Why don't you fight?" it demanded wrathfully of Rivera.

"You're yellow! You're yellow!" "Open up, you cur! Open up!" "Kill'm, Danny! Kill'm!" "You sure got'm! Kill'm!"

In all the house, bar none, Rivera was the only cold man. By temperament and blood he was the hottest-passioned there; but he had gone through such vastly greater heats that this collective passion of ten thousand throats, rising surge on surge, was to his brain no more than the velvet cool of a summer twilight.

Into the seventeenth round Danny carried his rally. Rivera, under a heavy blow, drooped and sagged. His hands dropped helplessly as he reeled backward. Danny thought it was his chance. The boy was at his mercy. Thus Rivera, feigning, caught him off his guard, lashing out a clean drive to the mouth. Danny went down. When he arose, Rivera felled him with a down-chop of the right on neck and jaw. Three times he repeated this. It was impossible for any referee to call these blows foul.

"Oh, Bill! Bill!" Kelly pleaded to the referee.

"I can't," that official lamented back. "He won't give me a chance."

Danny, battered and heroic, still kept coming up. Kelly and others near to the ring began to cry out to the police to stop it, though Danny's corner refused to throw in the towel. Rivera saw the fat police captain starting awkwardly to climb through the ropes, and was not sure what it meant. There were so many ways of cheating in this game of the Gringos. Danny, on his feet, tottered groggily and helplessly before him. The referee and the captain were both reaching for Rivera when he struck the last blow. There was no need to stop the fight, for Danny did not rise.

"Count!" Rivera cried hoarsely to the referee.

And when the count was finished, Danny's seconds gathered him up and carried him to his corner.

"Who wins?" Rivera demanded.

Reluctantly, the referee caught his gloved hand and held it aloft.

There were no congratulations for Rivera. He walked to his corner unattended, where his seconds had not yet placed his stool. He leaned backward on the ropes and looked his hatred at them, swept it on and about him till the whole ten thousand Gringos were included.

His knees trembled under him, and he was sobbing from exhaustion. Before his eyes the hated faces swayed back and forth in the giddiness of nausea. Then he remembered they were the guns. The guns were his. The Revolution could go on.

A Note About the Author

Jack London (1876–1916) was an American novelist and journalist. Born in San Francisco to Florence Wellman, a spiritualist, and William Chaney, an astrologer, London was raised by his mother and her husband, John London, in Oakland. An intelligent boy, Jack went on to study at the University of California, Berkeley before leaving school to join the Klondike Gold Rush. His experiences in the Klondike—hard labor, life in a hostile environment, and bouts of scurvy—both shaped his sociopolitical outlook and served as powerful material for such works as "To Build a Fire" (1902), *The Call of the Wild* (1903), and *White Fang* (1906). When he returned to Oakland, London embarked on a career as a professional writer, finding success with novels and short fiction. In 1904, London worked as a war correspondent covering the Russo-Japanese War and was arrested several times by Japanese authorities. Upon returning to California, he joined the famous Bohemian Club, befriending such members as Ambrose Bierce and John Muir. London married Charmian Kittredge in 1905, the same year he purchased the thousand-acre Beauty Ranch in Sonoma County, California. London, who suffered from numerous illnesses throughout his life, died on his ranch at the age of 40. A lifelong advocate for socialism and animal rights, London is recognized as a pioneer of science fiction and an important figure in twentieth century American literature.

A Note from the Publisher

Spanning many genres, from non-fiction essays to literature classics to children's books and lyric poetry, Mint Edition books showcase the master works of our time in a modern new package. The text is freshly typeset, is clean and easy to read, and features a new note about the author in each volume. Many books also include exclusive new introductory material. Every book boasts a striking new cover, which makes it as appropriate for collecting as it is for gift giving. Mint Edition books are only printed when a reader orders them, so natural resources are not wasted. We're proud that our books are never manufactured in excess and exist only in the exact quantity they need to be read and enjoyed. To learn more and view our library, go to minteditionbooks.com

bookfinity & MINT EDITIONS

Enjoy more of your favorite classics with Bookfinity,
a new search and discovery experience for readers.
With Bookfinity, you can discover more vintage
literature for your collection, find your Reader Type,
track books you've read or want to read,
and add reviews to your favorite books.
Visit www.bookfinity.com, and click on
Take the Quiz to get started.

Don't forget to follow us
@bookfinityofficial and @mint_editions

CPSIA information can be obtained
at www.ICGtesting.com
Printed in the USA
BVHW012119120322
631347BV00002B/38